Dear Reader,

Welcome to Encore Edition #1 in the series of *Great Lakes Romances*, historical fiction full of love and adventure set in bygone days on North America's vast inland waters.

Like the other books in this series, *Isabelle's Inning* relays the excitement and thrills of a tale skillfully told, but contains no explicit sex, offensive language, or gratuitous violence.

We invite you to tell us what you would like most to read about in *Great Lakes Romances*. For your convenience, we have included a survey form at the back of the book. Please fill it out and send it to us.

At the back, you will also find descriptions of other romances in this series, and a biography in the *Bigwater Classics* series, stories that will sweep you away to an era of gentility and enchantment, and places of unparalleled beauty and wonder!

Thank you for being a part of *Great Lakes Romances!*

Sincerely,
The Publishers

P.S. Author Donna Winters loves to hear from her readers. You can write to her at:

P.O. Box 177
Caledonia, MI 49316.

A SPECIAL NOTE

FROM AUTHOR

DONNA WINTERS

Due to the limited time frame for producing this story for my *Great Lakes Romances* series, I have chosen a wholly fictional setting which the reader can place anywhere in the lower Great Lakes region.

Keeping with the tradition of sharing authentic history in my stories, I have drawn on several reputable sources to relay the facts, atmosphere, and attitudes concerning the arrival of the automobile on our nation's roadways.

One exception, however, is the turn-of-the-century automobile shown on the back cover. This illustration is for artistic purposes only and not intended to represent either the 1903 Cadillac or 1901 Oldsmobile in *Isabelle's Inning*.

Isabelle's Inning

Donna Winters

Great Lakes Romances®

Bigwater Publishing
Caledonia, Michigan

Isabelle's Inning
Copyright c 1997 by Donna Winters

Encore Edition #1 is adapted from *Weatherby's Inning* by Ralph Henry Barbour
c 1903 by D. Appleton and Company

Great Lakes Romances is a registered trademark of Bigwater Publishing,
P.O. Box 177, Caledonia, Michigan 49316.

Library of Congress Catalog Card Number: 96-95157
ISBN 0-923048-85-5

Edited by Pamela Quint Chambers
Front cover art by C. M. Relyea (from the 1903 publication)

Printed in the United States of America

97 98 99 00 01 02 03 /   / 10 9 8 7 6 5 4 3 2 1

CHAPTER

1

As nineteen-year-old Isabelle Dorlon's buckboard bumped along River Street into Centerport her thoughts were not on the harbingers of an early spring that greeted her in the village—not on the scent of earth awakening that tinged hometown air or the delicate beauty of purple and yellow crocuses that bloomed in profusion along the drive curving up to the Jamison mansion.

Instead, her heart and mind lagged miles behind on the three business calls she and her mutt, Chips, had made on neighboring towns in Lakeshore County this unseasonably warm March day. Unable to follow maps and forgetful of verbal directions, Isabelle was pleased to think she had only lost her way twice.

But what delighted her far more than this were unexpectedly lucrative winter sales of the brooms bearing her brother's name, *T. Dorlon*. Demand had been strong enough to provide the funds for Tracy to pay off loans taken out in January for his final semester at Erskine College. Despite hardships since her father's death two years ago, the Lord had been faithful, and she silently thanked

Him that Tracy would be debt-free on his graduation day this spring.

Slowing at the intersection of Main, Isabelle was imagining the glow that would spread over her mother's face at the welcome financial news. No longer would she need to fill both dormer bedrooms with roomers from the college, provide training table meals for the entire baseball team from April till mid-June, or furnish backbreaking laundry service for students living far from home, and a ball team which often played on muddy fields. Next fall, Tilda Dorlon could sit on the porch, Chips at her feet, and take up fancywork at her leisure.

But the tranquil scene was supplanted by the sight of townsfolk streaming down Main Street toward the river. Quickly deciding to follow, Isabelle turned at the corner and drove the half block to the bridge to discover that it had been roped off. Throngs of the curious had gathered at the water's edge on either side. The river had already risen within inches of the bridge floor. The undertone of the swift spring current was accented by louder thuds of ice chunks battering ancient wooden supports as the river flowed ever more rapidly toward the big lake half a mile away.

Chips rose from the tarp on the bed of the buckboard and let out a low growl.

"Easy, boy," she comforted, stepping down from the driver's bench and inviting him to join her. The large mongrel leaped to the ground, staying close at her side as they found a place on the riverbank just downstream of the bridge. Nearby, a group of curious young boys jostled each other playfully for the best view. Jimmy Jamison, the son of the wealthiest man in town, was among them. Suddenly, he lost his footing and slid into the swift current. Thrashing the water wildly, he sent up a shrill appeal.

"Help! Somebody, *help!*"

Twenty-year-old Jack Weatherby, on his way home to Mrs. Dorlon's rooming house after spring baseball practice at Erskine College, was standing fifty yards downstream from the bridge on an as yet unflooded pier when he heard the cry for help. A young fellow splashed madly as the current carried him along. Then he disappeared for several seconds beneath the churning, gray waters. When he resurfaced, his energy was obviously fading.

Jack looked about frantically for a plank or a rope— anything he could offer the boy who would soon pass the pier. Finding nothing, he panicked with the knowledge that he was the youngster's only hope for help. Drawing back from the edge of the pier, his own black memories flooded his mind and froze his muscles.

The young boy surfaced near the pier, face pale, eyes dazed, lips silent.

The opportunity for rescue slipped by. The distance between the dock and the boy lengthened. Someone pushed past Jack, stripped off his jacket, and dove into the dangerous current. Stirring from his trance-like state, Jack recognized the rescuer as Tracy Dorlon, the captain and first baseman of the Erskine team on which Jack so desperately wanted a position as one of the nine.

Tracy cut through the raging river waters with bold strokes, caught hold of the boy's shirt collar, and began struggling upstream, approaching the pier a few minutes later.

Jack bent down and reached out to Tracy, barely aware

that others had joined him on the dock. Somewhere near-by, a dog barked furiously. Just when Jack expected Tracy's hand to grip his, he reached past him.

Isabelle Dorlon had come to her brother's rescue with a big, long pole. Instantly, Jack added his grip to hers, their hands overlapping on the thick hardwood staff. Together, they managed to haul Tracy and the limp boy up onto the dock, now thronged with students and townsfolk. The Dorlons' dog immediately began licking the boy's face.

With a disparaging glance at Jack, Tracy lifted the apparently lifeless body into his arms. Cutting a path through the crowd, he set a rapid pace for Isabelle's buckboard. Jack followed, keenly aware of others beside him muttering unkind remarks.

A young boy equal in age to the victim ran up to Jack and shook his finger in his face.

"Coward! You coulda saved my friend. It's your fault if he dies!"

The young boy ran after Tracy, pulling himself up into the bed of the buckboard and settling at the victim's side along with Chips and Isabelle. Tracy took the driver's seat and headed up Main Street toward Dr. White's office.

Following on foot, Jack sent up a desperate prayer that they would not be too late.

CHAPTER

2

Jack hadn't long to wait for the answer to his prayer. By the time he reached Dr. White's office, he could see through the half-open door of the examining room that the young lad was sitting up on the table, still coughing, but telling his account of his brush with death to his pal, Tracy and Isabelle, and the good doctor.

"There was a fellow on a pier, and . . . I thought for sure he'd pull me out. Then everything went blank, and . . . next thing I knew, I was being carried in here."

Jack stepped into the room to express his concern. But before he could speak, the young fellow stared and pointed.

"You're the fellow from the pier!"

The boy's friend eyed Jack with derision. "He's the coward all right, Jimmy! Never seen—"

Isabelle cut in quietly but firmly. "Tommy, enough." To the doctor, she said, "If you'll lend Jimmy a blanket, we'll drive him home directly. Mrs. Jamison is probably worried sick."

Jimmy shook his head. "Mama's not home. Neither is Papa."

Isabelle said, "Well, certainly *someone* is expecting

you."

Tommy grinned mischievously. "Yeah. His sister. Judith told Jimmy to be home by five, but he doesn't pay her any mind."

Isabelle wagged her finger. "Shame on you, Jimmy Jamison. You're very late. Come along, now."

Thankful that Jimmy had recovered, Jack slipped outside, intending to take off on foot for the Dorlons', when Isabelle caught up with him.

"You might as well ride with us, Mr. Weatherby. We're all headed for the same place."

Jack took a really good look at her for the first time since the incident on the pier. Several strands of dark hair were askew from her topknot. Her skirt was damp and rumpled from efforts to save Jimmy. And the narrow satin bow she always tied around the cuff of her right wrist had come undone. Despite all this, she possessed an innocent beauty that had attracted him since their first acquaintance in January.

And he would have accepted her invitation in an instant if not for the other riders who would accompany them. In no mood to be ridiculed further, he shook his head.

"I'll walk. Thanks anyway," he replied as Tracy and the boys emerged from the office.

Evidently over his pique, Tracy amicably ordered, "Pile in, Weatherby. You're riding with us."

Unwilling to argue further, he did as he was told, finding a none-too-comfortable place amongst Tommy, Jimmy, Chips, and the hardwood poles beneath the tarp on the bed of the buckboard.

En route to the Jamison mansion, Isabelle couldn't help

remembering three years back when she would walk there after lunch on Tuesdays and Thursdays to polish silver. The small job had paid nicely with the added benefit that Judith Jamison, a former classmate at the local grammar school, had apologized for her unkind taunts during their childhood when she and the other children had teased Isabelle over her father's broom making business.

"I'll bet your mother rides a broom on Halloween," they used to say.

Taunts aside, Isabelle could reflect fondly on the friendship which had begun to thrive a few years ago, then suffered a setback when her father had gone into a decline with a fatal blood disease. The tragedy had required Isabelle to give up her silver polishing and put constant efforts into two necessary endeavors—helping her mother start the rooming and boarding house, and learning the broom making business carried on in the work shed off the carriage house.

Recalling those difficult days and Judith's sincere concern, Isabelle concluded that their friendship would have deepened if not for Mrs. Jamison's decision to send Judith to a finishing school out East—likely in hopes of finding her plain-faced daughter a good marriage prospect. The plan evidently failed to produce the intended result, however, for when Isabelle encountered Judith in passing several weeks ago, she learned that her former friend had completed her schooling and no mention was made of an impending marriage. Now, as Tracy pulled into the long drive, Isabelle sent up a prayer of thanks that Judith's brother seemed none the worse for the mishap at the river.

In the minute required to climb the mild incline to the mansion, Isabelle had an opportunity to view up close the hundreds upon thousands of crocuses she had noticed from a distance earlier. She marveled at the shear effort of planting all those bulbs, a task that had undoubtedly fallen to a gardener and his assistants after Mrs. Jamison, president of the garden club, conceived the design.

As Tracy drew nearer the house, Isabelle realized the tiny blossoms helped soften the effect of the imposing Greek Revival façade. Its mighty pillars, dressed in a fresh coat of white paint, guarded black shutters of a magnificently large window, and through it Isabelle detected the figure of a tall, large-framed woman in motion.

Judith Jamison paced back and forth across the Persian rug, her focus fixed on the walkway visible from the front parlor window. Her brother should have come home from Tommy McGinty's house nearly an hour ago. When she had rung up Mrs. McGinty to remind Jimmy of that fact, she had learned that the boys had gone off to the store to purchase penny candy and had not yet returned. Mrs. McGinty seemed unconcerned.

"They paid a call on Mr. Overing at the cycle shop," she had said. "He's a storyteller, he is, and like as not, the boys lost track of time. They'll be along soon."

But Mrs. McGinty was wrong. Now, Judith was considering asking the hired man to go looking for Jimmy even though this was Mr. Herder's day off. She paused at the window to push back the creamy lace curtain for a better view.

A buckboard was coming up the driveway. She recognized Jimmy in the back, wrapped Indian-style in a blanket. Tracy Dorlon was driving, Isabelle beside him. Relief tussled with anger for control of Judith's emotions.

The moment the buckboard halted beneath the porte-cochère, Isabelle's old chum exited the beveled glass door, a reprimand on her lips.

"James Richard Jamison the Third, where on earth have you been? Do you realize—"

Tommy interrupted. "He nearly drowned in the river!" Hopping down, he was followed out of the buckboard by Jimmy, who shivered beneath his blanket while continuing the explanation.

"Mr. Tracy and . . . Miss Isabelle pulled me out!"

Judith focused on the Dorlons for the first time.

"Is that true?"

Before they could answer, she drew her own conclusion.

"It must be. Tracy, you're soaked! I'll be back in an instant with a blanket."

"No need," Tracy argued, but Judith seemed not to hear him as she escorted her brother into the house to the accompaniment of a thorough tongue-lashing.

A minute later, she returned, blanket in hand.

"My apologies, Tracy. I'm very sorry for the imposition. Please wrap yourself up before you catch your death." To Isabelle, she offered a smile and a warm greeting. "Good to see you again! Sorry it wasn't under better circumstances."

Isabelle nodded. "I'll return your blanket tomorrow."

Judith dismissed the offer with a wave of her hand. "I'll stop by for it after I return Jimmy's blanket to Dr. White, if it won't be an inconvenience. About four?"

"I'll be there," Isabelle promised.

Minutes later, she was thankful to finally arrive home.

As her brother pulled into the driveway of the ivory clapboard house with its green shuttered dormers and overhanging elms, she was reminded by contrast how vastly it differed from the perfectly-kept manor of the Jamison family.

By comparison, Dorlons' roof was in need of repair, and the front eaves were in want of a thorough spring cleaning. Autumn leaves and winter ice had taken their toll on them and the front porch as well, whose gray flooring and blue ceiling could do with fresh paint. She was consoled, however by the remembrance of her very successful business trip about the county earlier in the day. Now, she couldn't resist imagining her mother ensconced in a white wicker chair, needlepoint in hand, finally enjoying her long-deserved respite from household chores.

Her musings vanished as Tracy brought the buckboard to a halt in front of the carriage house. "Tell Mother that Weatherby and I will be in for dinner as soon as we put away the rig."

"Don't be long," Isabelle warned. "You know how she hates latecomers to the table. You'll need time to change into dry clothes, too."

He nodded as he helped her down, then handed her the Jamison's blanket and a satchel from beneath the seat. Chips jumped down from his place in the rear and followed her onto the back porch where she draped the damp blanket over a chair. Her dog's soft whine and soulful look at his empty dish reminded Isabelle that he'd gone without food the whole day long, and that a tasty treat, compliments of one of her business acquaintances, awaited him inside her bag. Quickly, she pulled out the paper-wrapped package.

Before she'd even untied the string, Chips was sniffing the parcel, licking his chops, and squealing softly in antici-

10

pation. She opened the paper flat and offered him a large, meaty beef bone. He gripped it in his powerful jaw and pranced off to his favorite spot beside the carriage house while she looked on with pleasure.

She was about to turn and enter the house when she remembered a another gift she'd left on the bed of the buckboard. Knowing of her mother's plans to serve pork this evening, she headed for the carriage house. She was brought up short outside the door by the sound of her brother's voice, low and taunting.

"When word gets out, your chances of making the nine are over. Tommy was right. You're really just a—"

Isabelle stepped through the door and interrupted her brother sharply. "Tracy, shame!" She shook her finger. "You're talking like a thirteen-year-old, except you should know better!"

"Stay out of this, Sis!"

"I will not!"

Jack was staring down at the straw-covered floor, his face crimson, his broad shoulders slumped. Isabelle's heart went out to him. With sympathy and an intuition she didn't fully understand, she continued. "I don't know exactly what happened to Mr. Weatherby on the pier today, but I suspect it had nothing to do with a lack of courage."

"Then what?" Tracy's burning gaze alternated between his sister and Jack.

Silence reigned. A silence during which Isabelle remembered the strength of Jack's hands covering hers on the pole as they pulled Tracy to the pier, then the ease with which he hauled first Jimmy, then her brother out of the river. An unbidden warmth washed over her, a warmth she had noticed upon their first meeting in January, and count-

11

less other occasions since.

When she spoke, her words quietly conveyed the charity she felt for the young man. "When Mr. Weatherby is ready, I'm sure he'll explain what really happened. In any case, the casting of negative aspersions serves no good purpose. Now, *please*—finish here as quickly as possible so you won't be late to the dinner table." Fetching the small can of maple syrup from beneath the tarp, she made haste for the back door.

Her mother's greeting was both surprising and nonchalant as she scooped mounds of mashed potatoes into a huge serving bowl.

"Thought you'd gotten lost till I heard you and Tracy were down to the river saving the life of Jimmy Jamison, the little rascal!" Her tone revealed pride and love as generous as the blue calico apron that covered her ample figure.

"How did you know?" Isabelle, wondered, setting the maple syrup on the counter.

"Anthony, Gregory, and Reginald were down to the bridge this afternoon." She named the other three roomers whose voices could be heard in conversation in the sitting room. "Said they saw you leaving Dr. White's about half past five. Is Tracy—"

"Tracy and Mr. Weatherby will be in from the carriage house momentarily," Isabelle explained as she quickly exchanged her wrap and hat for the apron on the wall peg by the door.

Using her spoon as a pointer, her mother indicated the maple syrup. "Where'd this come from?"

"It's a gift from Mr. Carter over in Gerrydale," Isabelle explained as she tied her apron strings.

Setting a dirty pot in the sink, Tilda Dorlon glanced at the tin again and frowned. "I hope that's not all you've got to show for your day of galavantin' about the county."

"Not by a far piece." Isabelle leaned close to her mother to speak in confidential tones about the lucrative nature of her day's efforts.

Tilda Dorlon broke into a wide smile. "I'm so proud of you! Your papa, rest his soul, would have been—"

"Don't say it, Mama," Isabelle warned, a pang like that of a sharp knife cutting through her. "You know how papa felt about me getting involved in his business."

Ignoring her daughter's remark, Tilda Dorlon pulled a piece of kindling from the box by the cast iron stove, used it to release the catch on the oven door, and removed the roast. The aroma of pork seasoned with garlic mingled with subtler hints of peas and onions still simmering on the back burner. Testing the meat for doneness with a large fork, she told Isabelle, "Everything's ready. We might as well serve up. If Tracy and Jack miss out, it's their own fault."

Mrs. Dorlon was asking the blessing by the time Tracy, in dry clothes, claimed his seat left of Jack and Isabelle at the dining table. When grace had ended, Gregory Stiles, best contender for catcher on the nine, wasted no time hailing Tracy the man of the hour.

"We saw you pluck that kid from a watery grave this afternoon. How does it feel to be the hero of all Centerport?"

Before Tracy could reply, Reginald Billings, the most likely candidate for pitcher, piped up. "Three cheers for Tracy! Hip, hip—"

Tilda Dorlon cut into the conversation from her place at the head of the table. "*Mr.* Billings, if you don't mind, any cheering will have to wait till dinner's over."

He smiled sheepishly. "Sorry, Mrs. Dorlon."

Accepting his apology with a nod, she said, "Come here. Since you're so full of enthusiasm, you can carve the roast this evening." She stood, ready to swap places.

Anthony Tidball, whose extra-curricular interests lay with the Lyceum and Erskine's debaters, and occasionally in parlor conversations and dog-walking with Isabelle, observed wryly, "Now you've done it, Billings."

Billings remained seated. "Trust me, Mrs. Dorlon. You don't want me to carve the meat."

She shrugged. "Guess we'll all go hungry, then."

Jeers from Gregory, Tracy, and Anthony soon convinced Reginald to comply with Mrs. Dorlon's request. Jack was keenly aware that when Reginald laid a slice of roast on his plate, it was considerably thinner than those cut for the others, and except for Anthony, the fellows sent neither a glance nor a word in his direction. Making matters worse were the sympathetic glances offered by Isabelle who evidently realized that the others were giving him the cold shoulder.

When the main course had ended and Mrs. Dorlon and Isabelle had returned to the kitchen to fetch dessert, Billings fastened a heated look of disgust on Jack, his taut words targeted for Tracy.

"Captain, you're not planning to allow a gutless fellow the likes of him on the team, are you?"

In a low voice, Stiles shared his own sentiments. "Because if you are, you'll be minus your catcher and pitcher from last season."

14

Jack didn't wait for Tracy's reply. Burning with humiliation, he tossed his napkin on his seat and made a swift exit through the back door, vaguely aware of the curious looks he earned from Mrs. Dorlon and Isabelle.

Outside, he paced up and down the driveway a few times, then toward the back of the yard, earning a growl from Chips who evidently felt the need to protect his bone. Preoccupied with the possibility of being banned from the baseball team before receiving a fair tryout, in his search for solitude, Jack inadvertantly headed directly for the door to the private work shed extending off the carriage house.

Forgotten were the instructions he'd been given his first day at the Dorlons' two months ago when his parents had helped him move in. The shed was strictly off limits to anyone but family. He'd noticed Isabelle and Tracy would spend hours there, and figured the reason for banning others was to prevent interruptions from whatever occupied them. Ignoring the warning, Jack slid back the heavy bolt on the door, taking refuge inside.

Grappling in the dark for a light, he'd no sooner found a string and pulled on it than a small, strong hand closed over his and extinguished the bulb in a flash.

The momentary glimpse of displeasure on Isabelle Dorlon's face and the shrill edge to her voice made him regret his intrusion.

"Mr. Weatherby! What in heaven's name do you think you're doing here?"

15

CHAPTER

3

When Jack offered not a single word of explanation for his presence in the work shed, Isabelle's fury heightened.

"Get out, Mr. Weatherby! Now!" In the darkness, she nudged him toward the door.

He put hands up. "Sorry! I'm going!"

Isabelle watched him head slowly for the house. Her anger subsiding, she recalled the reason she'd come looking for him in the first place. Bolting the door, she started after him, sympathy rising anew as she recalled Anthony's description of the scene that had unfolded while she and her mother had been in the kitchen cutting the custard pie. She caught up with Jack in the hazy light spilling off the back porch.

In as sweet a tone as she could muster, she asked, "Mr. Weatherby, may I have a word with you, please?"

When he faced her, a hurt, confused expression spoiled his firm jaw line and softened his normally confident gaze.

Eager to delay his return to the house, Jack paused to note not only the compassion he'd sensed in Isabelle at the dinner table, but a genuine contriteness on her face.

She spoke plainly. "I'm sorry about the way you were

treated at dinner. Anthony told Mother and me what was said to you while we were in the kitchen."

Too pained and embarrassed to discuss it, he switched topics. "I'm sorry about your work shed. No harm meant."

She accepted his apology with a nod. Calling Chips, she asked, "Could I impose upon you for a few minutes? I'd surely appreciate your company while I walk my dog."

Remembering that Anthony often walked with them, he asked, "Are you sure Mr. Tidball won't mind?"

"Anthony is preparing for a debate. I'll fetch Chips's leash."

Isabelle's use of Tidball's first name gave Jack pause. The two were evidently closer friends than he'd realized, raising a real concern that he could be stepping in where not wanted. He found little choice in the matter upon Isabelle's return with a leashed Chips. Full darkness had set in and he couldn't let her walk unescorted.

Chips led them across Elm Street to Monument Park, marking every hitching post, bush, and tree in the entire square, curiously avoiding the equestrian statue at the center, a tribute to a Union officer whose name meant nothing to Jack but was evidently prominent in Centerport's history.

Conversation consisted mostly of Isabelle's commands to her pet. A "Come along, Chips," when he spent too much time sniffing out the territory, and a sharp "Leave it!" when he spied a rabbit grazing on newly sprouted shoots in the tulip patch.

They'd exited the square and were headed for home when Isabelle spoke to Jack with a forthrightness he hadn't anticipated.

"Mr. Weatherby, what really *did* happen to you on the

17

pier today?"

Moments lapsed before he offered a subdued reply. "I'd rather not say." Halfway down the block, his curiosity triggered a question of his own. "Miss Dorlon, why is the shed off limits?"

The discreet smile that curved her pretty mouth revealed her answer even before her words did. "I'd rather not say."

The conversational stand-off lasted until they'd nearly reached the Dorlons' front walk when Isabelle spoke again.

"Anthony says if he wins only one debate this year, he's determined to beat Robinson next month. The Erskine debaters lost in a tight contest last year, and they're determined not to suffer another season of shame."

Jack, who had followed the keen rivalry between Erskine and Robinson on the ball diamond since he was a boy, had been unaware that the competition extended to the debaters, as well. "Will you go and lend him your support?"

She gave a tiny shake of her head, but the contemplative look in her wide-set eyes revealed more than her words. "Robinson's two hours away by train. I can ill afford either the time, or the fare."

"I understand Erskine's last baseball game this season is at Robinson. Maybe you can go then, to cheer on your brother."

Isabelle laughed. "I'll do as I did last year. Wait until he shows up at home to describe to Mother and me every play of the game, inning by inning. I'm convinced the telling of it is half my brother's fun!"

Remembering his own penchant for doing precisely the same with his cousin, Catherine, he replied, "So I've been

18

told."

As he held the front door, Isabelle stepped past him then released Chips from his leash. "Good night, Mr. Weatherby, and thanks."

Jack nodded, watching as her slim form disappeared down the dim hallway. Fragments of conversation came to him from upstairs. Billings and Stiles were discussing the big men of the Detroit Tigers—Charlie Carr and Punkins Kissinger—and their recent arrival in Shreveport for a series of preseason games. The sound of Reginald's and Gregory's voices reminded Jack that he was unready to return to his own room next to theirs. Quietly, he slipped out the front door and headed for Erskine's campus.

His feet carried him to the ball diamond. Approaching home plate, he crouched as if at bat, took a few practice swings, and waited for the imaginary first pitch to be thrown. Swinging hard, he could feel the vibration of the bat connecting with the ball, and hear its crack. A line drive sailed far into the outfield. He saw himself streaking around the bases.

He wandered over to the bench where the Erskine nine would sit at every home game and took a place near the center. His eight-year goal of playing on the team was about to wash down the river along with his reputation. He wondered why he had made so many sacrifices to get here—taking part time jobs, saving his money, attending a less expensive school for the first two years of college—if his dream could drown so quickly.

Perhaps he should go home, save himself the expense of attending Erskine. To stay and not play would be worse. Gazing at the stands, he knew he didn't want to sit up there and watch the team which had captured his loyalty all those years ago in a shut-out against Robinson College. He wanted to sit right here, on the bench, in the batting line-up. To be anything less than a part of the action was simply unacceptable.

Those thoughts took flight as the slightly stooped figure of the groundskeeper, Thaddeus Tuttle—Mr. T to the students—approached along the third base line in his unhurried gait. Groaning slightly as he took a place beside Jack on the bench, he spoke in the same gruff voice Jack had heard time and again when he greeted fellows coming on the field for practice.

"Seen ya a few minutes ago at the plate, swingin' a bat that don't exist, hittin' a pitch that ain't been thrown." He cleared his throat with a deep, rumbling sound, his next words surprisingly tender. "What's the matter, son? Are ya worried ya might not be good enough to make the team?"

Jack yearned to tell Mr. T what had happened since he'd left practice that afternoon—yearned to explain the unfair treatment being dealt him by the other players rooming at Dorlons'—but he would sound like a whiner. Instead, he simply nodded.

"In thirty years, I seen many a ball player strugglin' through spring practice on Erskine field. Some were better 'n you, some not as good. There's one thing I can tell ya for sure. Since Coach Hanson come here ten years ago, every fella tryin' out for the Erskine nine gets a fair chance."

His words breathed new life into the dying flicker of hope in Jack's heart. Perhaps skill alone would determine the team roster, not the aspersions ignorantly cast by others.

The groundskeeper continued. "'Tweren't always so. I

remember the first year I come to work here, 'way back in '73 . . . "

Jack's mind wandered from the story Mr. T was telling to his own route to Erskine College, a journey that had begun when he was twelve. Away from the family farm for a stay with his city cousins, Jack watched Erskine's Purple Stockings beat Robinson's Brown Stockings in a competition which had included a grand slam in the ninth inning. From that time on, he had carried a dream of playing on the Erskine nine. Prayers, practices, hard work, and God's grace had prepared him for it, first by playing ball on his grammar school team, then moving in with his aunt, uncle, and cousins in River Bend to attend high school and play baseball there.

After graduation, when his cousins Catherine and Clifford were making plans for schooling out East, Jack dreamed of attending Erskine, but finances were insufficient. His aunt and uncle, knowing how much they would miss their own children, suggested he continue to live with them and enter the city's two-year business school, then move on to Erskine. Jack remembered how, though the small school had no baseball team, the Lord had led him to a job that kept him in practice and helped him save for Erskine—a position as the assistant to his high school coach.

His reminiscing ended upon Mr. T's mention of a name with a familiar ring.

" . . . Whittaker. Played here from '75 to '79. Best catcher ever squatted 'hind Erskine's home plate. Coulda played for Cincinnati, but—"

Jack interrupted. "Are you talking about Judge Whittaker in River Bend?"

"'At's right."

21

Fond remembrances made Jack smile. "He was my next door neighbor for the last six years! He played catch with me for hours in the back yard."

"Didn't know ya was from River Bend."

"I wasn't. I lived there with my aunt and uncle."

Mr. T smiled wryly. "Last time I seen Judge Whittaker all he could talk about was his '01 Oldsmobile."

Jack laughed. "He's mighty fond of it."

Mr. T cleared his throat and resumed his reminiscences. "Year after Whittaker left Erskine, a pitcher name of Haskins showed up . . . "

With interest, Jack listened to a litany of success stories —some about players who were skilled from the start, and others about athletes who were weak in their first spring practice but worked hard enough to make it to the National League after college and Western League experience.

" . . . so ya see, son, anythin's possible if y'r willin' to work hard enough." He clapped Jack on the shoulder. "See ya tomorrow at practice."

Jack watched him shuffle off, his thoughts returning to the scene on the pier at the river, and the real reason for his dilemma. Despite Hanson's reputation for fairness, Jack worried that the man could be swayed, seeing him the object of insults and scorn by his peers—and with less than two weeks of practice to go before the team roster would be posted!

He slipped off the bench, onto his knees, and with head bowed, sent up a quiet prayer. "Lord, You know how badly I want to play on the Erskine nine. I can't give up baseball now—unless You want me to. Show me what I should do. Thy will, not mine. Amen."

Remaining on his knees in silent meditation, he listened

to an inner voice, words of wisdom not his own. The recollection of a Bible verse reminded him that *all things are possible*. With a new purpose, he rose and headed home, God's direction and assurances squarely before him.

The hours before Judith Jamison's arrival seemed to pass all too swiftly for Isabelle. The morning was occupied by work in the shed, as was often her custom. After a light midday meal, she assisted her mother with laundry and cleaning chores.

Anthony returned from classes at three and disappeared behind the closed door to his room. Half an hour later, when Isabelle needed access for cleaning, she knocked, waited, then opened the door, recognizing the serious challenge before her. Not only were Anthony's books and papers strewn across every available surface, but he was so hard at work at his desk, he didn't even know she was there. Reluctant to disturb him but determined to carry on with her cleaning, she cleared her throat.

"Excuse me, Anthony. I'm sorry to interrupt you but there's something I'd like to ask."

He took off his glasses and greeted her with a half-smile. "Isabelle, I didn't hear you come in. What is it you'd like to know? Something pertaining to the internal combustion engine, I hope, because my mind's a blank on just about everything else right now."

She chuckled. "My topic is much simpler than that. I was wondering if you'd like to take a break from your studies and join mother and me for tea. An old friend is stopping by soon, and it would do you good to get out of your room for a few minutes."

He shook his head. "I'm not much for socializing.

Besides, I have a lot of work ahead of me before the debate at Robinson next month." Donning his glasses, he returned to his studies.

Faced with the continuing necessity of cleaning an occupied room, and reluctant to say more, Isabelle entered phase two of her ways to roust Anthony from his chair and draw him out of his room. Without a word, she headed downstairs. When she returned, Chips was leading the way, wearing his leash and carrying the handle in his mouth. He bounded into Anthony's room, placing his paws on the scholar's thigh.

Anthony greeted the mutt with a smile, ruffling him behind the ears. "Are you trying to tell me it's time for a walk?"

Chips barked in reply, his entire rear end wagging in anticipation.

Setting eyeglasses aside, Anthony asked Isabelle, "Care to join us for a turn around the block?"

Taking dust mop in hand, she waved them off. "You two go on, I need to clean up in here."

Finishing quickly in Anthony's room, Isabelle put away her cleaning supplies and with the help of her mother, set a tray with the best china tea set from the corner cabinet. Slicing a lemon, spreading a plate with ginger snaps, and pouring hot water over carefully measured tea leaves, she was prepared for Judith when the Jamison carriage came to a halt in front of the house.

Carrying the tea tray to the parlor, Isabelle was pleased to see from the front window that the return of Anthony and Chips had coincided with the arrival of her guest—so perfectly that on their way to the front door, they were already striking up a conversation. She hurried to let them in.

"Judith, welcome. I see you've already met Anthony Tidball, one of our roomers."

"Not formally," Judith replied. Offering Anthony her hand, she said, "Mr. Tidball, pleased to meet you."

Anthony tipped his head. "My pleasure, Miss . . . "

Isabelle spoke up. "Jamison. Her brother, Jimmy, was the one who fell into the river yesterday."

Still holding Judith's hand, Anthony asked, "And how is the lad today?"

"Fine except for a case of the sniffles, which is the very least he deserves for the scare he gave everyone," she replied, releasing her hand—though Isabelle thought reluctantly—to unfasten the frog of her forest green woolen cape.

Anthony released Chips from his leash, quickly removed his coat, and focused on Judith again. "I'll take your wrap, Miss Jamison. I'm on my way to the closet anyway." To Isabelle, he said, "Is it too late to change my mind about tea?"

Coming from the back of the house to join the others, Tilda Dorlon answered for her daughter. "Not at all. You young people go into the parlor and make yourselves comfortable." Reaching for the wraps and the leash Anthony was holding, she said, "I'll put these away and fetch an extra cup and saucer."

A minute later, Tilda returned. Helping Isabelle pass the tea and ginger snaps all around, she stayed but a few minutes to inquire of Judith's folks, then excused herself to commence dinner preparations.

During the quiet moment that followed, Isabelle took up the burden for conversation. "Judith, Mr. Tidball is the president of the Lyceum. He's been studying day and night for a debate next month at Robinson."

Judith smiled with interest. "What is the topic of your debate, Mr. Tidball?"

Swallowing the last of a ginger snap, he cleared his throat to reply in a lofty, confident tone, "The horseless carriage will replace the horse and carriage." He paused to add, "I'm taking the affirmative, in case you hadn't guessed."

Judith's face lit up, her words tumbling out. "Mr. Tidball, you simply *must* meet my father! He believes as you do. In fact, he's taking delivery of a Cadillac next week!"

Anthony drew a sharp breath. "Do you think . . . would he . . . "

"I'm sure he'd take you for a ride."

"I'd be ever so grateful. When will—"

"The automobile is due in on Tuesday's evening train. But I'll warn you, delivery has been postponed twice already, so don't be disappointed if it doesn't arrive."

Anthony pulled a notebook and pen from his inside pocket and mumbled while he scribbled. "Tuesday, the evening train. A horseless carriage delivered right here to Centerport." Shoving notebook and pen into his pocket, he focused on Judith again. "Do you realize how valuable this will be to my research, Miss Jamison?"

"I—"

Too excited to listen to her reply, he sprang to his feet. "Now, if you'll excuse me, I must return to my studies. Good day, Miss Jamison. It's been a pleasure!"

The thud, thud of Anthony taking the stairs two at a time put a smile on Isabelle's face. She told Judith, "I haven't seen Anthony this enthusiastic since he moved in last fall."

A wrinkle marred Judith's forehead. "I hope I haven't set him up for disappointment. Like I said, it's anybody's guess whether the thing will actually arrive Tuesday, or a month from Tuesday."

"God willing, for Anthony's sake, it will be sooner, rather than later," Isabelle replied, reaching for the teapot. "More?"

Consulting the watch pinned to the lapel of her mint green wool suit, Judith said, "I shouldn't overstay my welcome, but it's been such a long while since we've talked, it would be nice to catch up."

Isabelle filled both their cups, and kept refilling them until the teapot was empty and conversation had exhausted a wide range of topics. When Judith spoke ruefully of her failure to strike a rapport with any suitable young men out East, Isabelle made herself the object of conversation, bringing shared laughter over the times she had gotten lost going from one floor to another in the Jamisons' sprawling mansion, or stumbled over furniture that was constantly being rearranged.

She spoke, too, of broom making, her mother's rooming and boarding house business, and Tracy's captaincy of the Erskine nine. Dinner hour approaching, she fetched Judith's cape and the blanket which had been loaned to Tracy, and saw her friend to the foyer.

Judith paused just inside the front door. "Thank you for the tea and cookies. I've really enjoyed our time together. We'll talk again, when Father's horseless carriage—"

Her words were interrupted when Jack Weatherby burst through the front door, nearly knocking Judith down.

"Sorry! So sorry!" he mumbled. As he restored Ju-

27

dith's balance, Isabelle couldn't help noticing a large cut on his lower lip, already beginning to swell.

"Mr. Weatherby, you're hurt! What happened?"

Covering his mouth with his hand, he sprinted up the stairs without a word.

CHAPTER

4

Jack could ignore the stinging sensation in his lip as he sat down to dinner, but he could *not* ignore the question Tilda Dorlon posed the moment she took her place at the head of the table.

"Mr. Weatherby, have you been in a fight?"

His gaze meeting hers, he quietly replied, "No, ma'am."

Lines of suspicion ruling her forehead, she asked, "Would you please explain, then, how you got your swollen lip?"

He lowered his focus to the glistening china plate before him, the gazes of Tracy, Reginald, and Gregory burning into him. "I . . . I'd rather not say, ma'am, but I haven't been fighting."

Tilda sighed. "I'll take you at your word, but let me warn you fellows—and this includes you, Tracy. I offer room and board here for upstanding Christian men." Her voice grew stern. "Hooligans, brawlers, ruffians, and thugs are *not* welcome. If I see any more cut lips, a black eye, a bruised jaw, or other evidence of fisticuffs, you'll be out of this house on your ear. Understood?"

"Yes, ma'am," came a mumbled chorus in reply.

"Now that that's understood, Mr. Weatherby, it's your

turn to do the carving. Would you be so kind as to take my place at the head of the table and serve up the ham?"

Rising from his chair, he caught a glimpse of Isabelle. The disappointment—or perhaps it was disbelief—darkening her countenance sent a stabbing pain through him that trivialized the discomfort of his battered lip.

Taking meat fork and carving knife in hand he tried to shove the feeling aside. But as Anthony Tidball launched into an announcement about a motor car coming to Centerport, he wondered why Isabelle's opinion should affect him so.

When Tracy and the other fellows came bounding down the stairs the following Tuesday morning for breakfast and parked their books on the table in the hallway, Isabelle couldn't help noticing that Jack alone was carrying a canvas bag full of baseballs and a bat along with his texts and notebooks. When all had been seated at the table and the scrambled eggs and bacon strips passed around, he revealed the reason.

"Mrs. Dorlon, don't expect me for dinner this evening. I'll be staying later than usual at the ball field to practice my hitting."

She nodded appreciatively. "I'll plan accordingly, Mr. Weatherby."

Anthony spoke up. "You'll be at the depot at half-past six, won't you? Mr. Jamison's 1903 Cadillac is coming in."

Before Jack could reply, Tracy told Anthony, "The way you talked it up on campus, I won't be surprised if the whole student body shows up to see it. Coach Hanson even canceled baseball practice!"

Setting aside her glass of milk, Isabelle said, "When I was in Reilly's General Merchandise yesterday, Mr. Reilly told me customers were talking about it all last weekend. He thinks the whole town will turn out."

Billings said, "No offense, Tidball, but I don't see how gasoline powered engines are going to replace horses."

Stiles chuckled. "Reggie's right. Last summer I heard a motor car go past my folks' place. It sounded like a lunatic with a rifle running down the road!"

Despite laughter from the others, Anthony remained undaunted. "Some improvements are in order, but I maintain that over time, the internal combustion engine will prove itself reliable and practical. And I aim to be at the depot for its historic introduction to Centerport!"

Before further opinions could be aired, Tilda Dorlon took control of the conversation once again.

"Gentlemen, since your baseball practice has been canceled, and I, too, would like to be at the depot this evening upon the train's arrival, dinner will be served one quarter hour earlier than usual—at five forty-five. That will give all of us the opportunity to walk down to the station in plenty of time."

Throughout the morning, as Isabelle worked in the shed, then helped her mother with the ironing, she kept wondering what the arrival of the motor car could mean for Centerport, and whether indeed the whole population of the town would turn out to see it. Other subjects challenged her mind as well. A recurring image over the last few days had been that of Jack Weatherby on the dock the day Jimmy Jamison fell in the river. She shared her troubling thoughts about the incident with her mother, whose opinion raised a suggestion.

By dinner time, Isabelle had evolved a plan to put that suggestion into action. When the meal ended, Anthony, Gregory, Reginald, and Tracy excused themselves to head off to the depot.

As Isabelle carried a tray full of dirty dishes into the kitchen, her mother told her, "Just stack them by the sink, we'll wash them later. Let's be off, or we'll miss the arrival of the train." She took her shawl from the peg by the back door, then handed Isabelle her cape.

Donning her wrap, Isabelle reached for Chips's leash, which brought him barging out from his corner by the pantry. "I'm going to walk Chips over to the college instead, and watch Mr. Weatherby practice."

Her mother nodded. "Taking up that idea we discussed this afternoon, are you?"

Isabelle smiled. "Say a prayer for me."

Ten minutes later Isabelle arrived at the college. Students, faculty, and townsfolk had passed her streaming in the opposite direction, and now the campus was deserted—of all but one lone batsman on the ball diamond at home plate, and an array of balls in all parts of the field. She came up behind Jack who remained unaware of her presence until she unleashed Chips to chase a ball he'd sent sailing into left field.

His greeting was courteous but cool. "Miss Dorlon, I thought you'd be at the depot."

Watching Chips bound from one ball to another, unable to decide which to retrieve, she laughed. "And I thought you could use a good fielder, but I can see I've overestimated Chips's abilities."

Jack turned to watch the dog. His entertaining antics on

the field evidently tempered Jack's pique over the unwanted interruption, making him smile. Laying aside his bat, he
picked up his empty canvas bag. "Guess I'd better fetch the
balls myself."

Joining him on the field, Isabelle did her best to teach
Chips to pick up the balls then drop them into Jack's bag.
Though he was an ace at finding them, he was reluctant to
give them up, making soft growls when she tried to take
them from him, then circling about with the sought-after
prize clasped tightly in his jaw. Eventually, all the baseballs
were collected and Jack returned to home plate to resume
his hitting practice.

Feeling somewhat self-conscious with Isabelle looking
on, Jack tossed up the first ball, swung hard, and missed.
His second try sent a high ball toward second base. Chips
dashed out to fetch it, and with Isabelle's coaxing, eventually brought it to Jack and dropped it at his feet.

The routine continued until Jack saw Mr. T approaching with a familiar, broad-shouldered gentleman in a
Derby. Laying down his bat, Jack started down the third
base line to greet his former neighbor.

"Judge Whittaker, what are you doing in Centerport?"

A wide smile split his thick gray mustache from his
bushy beard. "Just checking on my favorite ball player!"
He hugged Jack's shoulders. "How's it going, son? I
thought the whole team would be out here practicing."

"Coach Hanson canceled practice for today."

Mr. T explained. "He an' all the other fellas 've gone to
the depot. An automobile's comin' in on the six-thirty
from Detroit."

The judge laughed. "I was wondering why the crowd
was so thick at the station." With a nod in the direction of

Isabelle and Chips, he said, "I see you have a couple of friends with you."

"Come on. I'll introduce you."

When Jack had acquainted Isabelle and Chips with both gentlemen, he told her, "Judge Whittaker has an '01 Oldsmobile. He used to take me all over River Bend in it. He even let me drive it a couple of times!"

The judge said, "That machine's now retired to my carriage house."

Isabelle said, "I'm sorry. You're probably quite disappointed that it doesn't run anymore."

Before the judge could say more, Mr. T said, "That don't surprise me none. Motor machines ain't never gonna outlast a good horse."

A twinkle in his eye, the judge explained, "My '01 still runs as good as the day I bought her. The only reason I put her away is because I'm driving a new model now—an '03 Curved Dash Runabout!"

A furrow deepened in Mr. T's brow. "Now what in tarnation would ya want with a new automobile when ya already got one that's runnin' perfectly good?"

The judge grinned. "When I decide in favor of something, I have a tendency to get downright fanatical!"

When all had laughed, Jack said, "Seems a shame no one's making using of the '01."

The judge nodded. "I'm planning to auction her off, or hold a raffle. I just haven't had time." He checked his watch. "Speaking of time, I'd better be on my way, or I'll miss the train home."

Mr. T said, "You be sure an' stop by next time ya come through Centerport!"

Whittaker replied, "You can count on it!" Jostling

Jack's shoulder, he said, "Practice hard. I expect to see you on the field when the Erskine nine come to River Bend a couple of months from now." To Isabelle, he said, "Pleasure to meet you, Miss Dorlon."

With a tip of his Derby, he headed back down the third base line with Mr. T.

As if on cue, Chips picked a ball out of Jack's athletic bag, dropped it at his feet, and went down on his front paws, barking playfully.

Jack stooped to pick it up, hit it into the field, and repeated the process dozens of times with Chips retrieving. When dusk had descended, he gathered his equipment, books, and the jacket he'd laid aside while at bat, telling Isabelle, "I guess it's time we all head home."

"Mr. Weatherby, before we go, I'd be most appreciative if you'd sit and talk a minute. There's something I've been meaning to ask you." She fiddled with the powder blue satin ribbon tied about the right cuff of her white blouse.

"There's something I've been meaning to ask you, too," he said offhandedly. "Why is it you always wear a colored ribbon on your wrist?"

"On my *right* wrist," Isabelle amended, hesitated, then plunged ahead. "I'm ashamed to admit I forget which is my right, and which is my left." She laughed unconvincingly.

"That answers that," he said lightly. Laying aside his paraphernalia, he sat down at an angle. "Now what did you want to ask me?"

She offered a nervous smile. Focusing on the strong, pleasing lines of his countenance, she tried to ignore the quickening of her pulse that raced faster as she delivered her next words.

"Mr. Weatherby, I've thought back many times to that day on the pier and the look of terror on your face, and I'm wondering . . . Don't you know how to swim?"

He gazed into her pretty, wide-set eyes. Feelings of shame made him long to look away, but he held his focus while recalling his prayer of a few nights ago. The Lord had reminded him that *all things are possible*.

He replied forthrightly. "No, Miss Dorlon, I don't know how to swim. But I intend to learn. In fact, I've been meaning for days now to ask your brother if he could help me, but—"

"*I* can help you!"

"You?"

Isabelle chuckled. "Don't look so surprised. I've been swimming like a fish since the age of five when I took it upon myself to swim out to the raft my brother and his friends had anchored at the lagoon near the big lake."

Recognizing an answer to prayer and an opportunity to fulfill his promise to do God's will, Jack said, "Miss Dorlon, I accept your offer of swimming lessons. But if you don't mind," he paused to pull on his jacket, "I'd prefer to wait for better weather."

Isabelle's laughter cascaded over him, warming his heart like no jacket could. "You'll get no argument from me on that score, Mr. Weatherby." Rising, she added, "Now, I'd be delighted to take you up on your offer to walk me home. Goodness knows, a mountain of work is waiting for me, but before I tackle it, I'll get you a sandwich. By now, you must be famished!" She moved away.

This time it was Jack who stalled, taking hold of her elbow to turn her toward him. On his brow was an unmistakable mark of apprehension.

"Miss Dorlon, there is one favor I'd like to ask. Could we keep the swimming lessons just between us? The other fellows—they don't know I can't—"

"I understand," she hastened to assure him. "The first warm Saturday, I'll pack a picnic lunch. We'll tuck our towels and swimming togs beneath the tarp on the buckboard and no one will be the wiser."

Anthony Tidball set such a rapid pace for the station that Tracy, Reginald, and Gregory soon lagged far behind despite their athletic prowess. A crowd had already begun to gather on the platform, but Anthony had no difficulty locating the Jamison family, all decked out in dusters.

Judith eagerly introduced Anthony to her parents and younger brother. Meeting them now, he recognized in Judith the square jaw and broad shoulders of her portly father, and the tall, angular figure and prominent nose of her mother.

Mr. Jamison regarded him with friendly skepticism. "Judith tells me you'll be expounding on the future of the horseless carriage in a debate at Robinson next month."

"Yes, sir!" he replied, perhaps too enthusiastically. "Anything I can learn about the gasoline powered automobile would be of great value."

"There's a world of difference between the various makes of automobiles," James Jamison cautioned. "Take the Cadillac, for instance. It has—"

Unable to restrain himself, Anthony cut in. "I know all about the Cadillac, sir. The factory sent me their literature. It features—"

This time, it was Jimmy who interrupted. "Look! The train's coming!"

Mr. Jamison gazed down the track. "So it is! And my motor car had better be on it or Henry Leland will get an earful from me!" he exclaimed, naming the originator of the Cadillac design.

His threat soon proved groundless, for when the train pulled into the station, a flatcar carrying a shrouded form the shape of a buggy was very much in evidence. A wiry fellow toting a mechanic's kit painted with the word "Cadillac" in stylized script hopped aboard the flatcar and began loosening the shroud. Scores of onlookers were gathering as Mr. Jamison cut a path through their midst, followed by Anthony and the rest of the Jamison family.

Evidently familiar with the factory man, Jamison greeted him as he stepped onto the flatcar to assist. "Chambers! It's about time you delivered!" To Anthony, he said, "Come up here, son, and give us a hand."

Within moments they had unknotted the cords. Playing the scene with all the drama of a theater actor, Jamison instructed Anthony and the mechanic to step back.

The crowd grew silent. Hundreds of eyes focused on Jamison.

He bent down, lifted one corner of the shroud a few inches, then lowered it again, offering his audience a sly smile.

The crowd mumbled. Judith spoke boldly.

"For goodness sakes, Father, take it off!"

With a sweeping, bold flourish, Jamison whipped away the cover.

There, glistening in the low-angled rays of sunset, stood a bright red wooden-bodied buggy. It sported two open seats of black tufted leather, spoked wheels with large rubber tires, and four red metal fenders for protection from dirt and mud. A steering wheel with a bulb horn had been mounted on the left in front, and two wicker baskets flanked either side of the rear seat. Two brass lamps graced the front end of the vehicle with one more at the rear.

But the feature that interested Anthony the most was mounted horizontally in the frame—the one-cylinder, water-cooled engine built by Leland and Faulconer. It boasted a five-inch bore and stroke giving a total piston displacement of 98.2 cubic inches, and an ignition by spark plug and high-tension coil.

Two freight haulers came to attached a wooden ramp to the flatcar. As the crowd pressed ever closer, Chambers expressed his concern.

"Ladies and gentlemen, please clear the way so I can drive the buggy off the train."

Mr. Jamison rested his hand on the mechanic's shoulder. "I'll drive it down the ramp, Chambers."

"Sir, with all due respect, I'd prefer to do it for you."

Jamison chuckled. "Don't you think I know how to handle that thing? I drove a Cadillac all around River Bend just last week—one that belongs to a friend of mine over there."

"But, sir—"

"You just leave the driving to me. After all, I paid the Cadillac Automobile Company $850 of my hard-earned money for the privilege." He stepped into the buggy and settled behind the wheel. "Tell me when you're ready for contact."

Drawing an uneasy breath, Chambers inserted the handle onto a crankshaft amidships and slowly turned over the engine once, then once again. Signaling to Jamison for contact, he cranked hard.

Immediately, the engine sprang to life. The automobile leaped forward, charged down the ramp, and shot straight ahead toward dozens of curious bystanders!

CHAPTER

5

At the sight of the runaway automobile, a woman shrieked. A father snatched his son from the path of the oncoming vehicle. Others scrambled to clear the way.

The Cadillac let out a deafening crack like canon fire.

Two horses bolted, galloping off with an empty runabout. Onlookers scrambled to get out from under foot.

Mr. Jamison and his automobile came to an abrupt halt twenty yards from where they'd started.

Anthony and the mechanic rushed to the scene, Judith close behind. She wagged her finger at her father. "Shame on you! You should have listened to Mr. Chambers!"

The mechanic spoke up. "Sir, you forgot to retard the spark."

Jamison scowled. "You forgot to remind me!" His frown turning into a grin, he said, "No harm done. Now, I'm going to take my family for a drive. Chambers, crank the thing up again." Beckoning to his wife, he settled her in the front seat beside himself. To Anthony and Judith, he said, "You two get in back."

Anthony helped Judith through the rear entrance to the tonneau.

Jimmy stood by the left front fender and whined. "Father, what about me?"

"Climb up here, son. We'll squeeze you in somehow."

Remembering this time to retard the spark, he signaled Chambers. One crank brought the Cadillac to life again. The engine chugged. Exhaust fumes drifted up.

Anthony inhaled deeply. "Ah, the sweet perfume of the mechanical age!"

Judith wrinkled her nose. "The horrid stench, you mean. This engine smells worse than a street full of horse droppings!"

Anthony made no reply, focusing now on the fact that the automobile was beginning to move, slowly accelerating as Mr. Jamison adjusted a lever that opened the inlet valve. He pulled out onto Railroad Street, turned right on Main, then headed up through town toward the college.

Anthony's heart skipped a beat at the realization that he was sitting in the back of a buggy unneedful of horses riding straight through the heart of Centerport. When he glanced at Judith, he could see from the look of wonder in her blue eyes that she had forgotten about the stink of exhaust fumes and was now in a state of pure amazement. He reached for her hand, giving it a nervous squeeze. She returned the affection, then pulled away, lowering her gaze. The rosy blush that flooded her cheeks could have resulted from the abrasion of the wind blowing through the open-air carriage, but he suspected its roots sprang from an entirely different chemistry—one of warmth within. At least he prayed it was so.

When Jack arrived home from the college ball field, Isabelle more than kept her promise to make him a sandwich. Included on the tray with his corned beef on rye were a large wedge of pecan pie and a tall glass of milk. He carried the meal up to his room where he eagerly devoured the supper before sitting down to tackle his studies.

From his desk by the window overlooking the back yard, he had a clear view of the carriage house and work shed. Tonight, like so many evenings past, when Isabelle finished helping her mother in the kitchen, she headed out there. Also, as in the past, once she had switched on the light that spilled through the windows of the work shed, Tracy could be heard descending the stairs. Moments later, Jack watched him cross the back yard to join his sister, text books bundled beneath his arm.

Jack wondered why Tracy would go there to study, rather than staying in his room. Recalling Isabelle's distress when he'd entered there by accident, he was curious as to what might be contained within besides the family broom making business. Once, when Tracy had dropped a book on the way to school, some papers had fallen out. When Jack had retrieved them for Tracy, he couldn't help noticing the beautiful penmanship—handwriting so tidy no man could have done it. Jack wondered if Isabelle was responsible for writing out Tracy's assignments while he worked on his brooms. He decided to challenge her with these questions when the opportunity arose.

He discovered his chance the following Sunday afternoon, offering to accompany her and Chips on their daily walk. They crossed the street to Monument Park where the benches remained vacant due to the stiff, cool breeze that was blowing in off the big lake.

Finding a location somewhat sheltered by a large elm, he said, "Miss Dorlon, could we sit a minute? There's something I've been wanting to ask you."

She settled on the bench and smiled up at him expectantly. "Is it about swimming? I don't know any fancy strokes, just the usual one." Patting Chips, she continued, "Now, dogs, on the other hand, do a sort of paddle. Chips is excellent—"

"It's not about swimming," Jack interrupted.

"Oh," she replied, falling silent.

"It's about the work shed."

"The work shed?"

"Yes. I'm wondering what you do out there besides broom making."

"Nothing," she replied too quickly to be convincing.

"Then why is the shed off limits to everyone except family? And why does Tracy take his books with him when he goes out to work on his brooms?"

Obviously stuck for a reply, Isabelle's gaze fled from Jack to the leash she held in her lap.

He continued. "Here's what I think. You're writing out Tracy's college assignments while he works on the brooms."

Her head snapped up. Cheeks draining of color, she regarded him through a curtain of ice, her words colder than the arctic. "Mr. Weatherby, you couldn't be more wrong."

She rose from the bench so swiftly, she nearly stumbled over Chips as she hauled him away.

When Jack finished breakfast the following Tuesday—the last day of March—he realized much to his regret that the warm-up in the weather over the past forty-eight hours had had no effect at all on Isabelle's coolness toward him. She barely returned his greetings when he sat down to the table. She passed dishes to him at dinner the night before without ever meeting his gaze, and she purposely focused on the floor when passing him in the hallway the previous afternoon.

Although her behavior was a sincere cause for regret, he spent little time worrying about it. His focus instead centered on the all-important last day of baseball practice before the varsity roster would be named. Picking up his bag of gear and his books, he headed out the door, anticipation of the four o'clock practice his only thought as he walked the short distance to campus.

Try as he might, he could barely concentrate on classes that day, which seemed to creep by slower than a slug in a stupor. When four o'clock finally arrived, he was the first to enter the locker room, the first to head out onto the field, and the first to begin the warm-up ritual.

Taking three laps around the bases, he became aware that the sun was shining brightly again, just like it had the day before. The field—muddy for so much of the past month—had turned green and springy. And the air bore a hint of a fresh water breeze coming in off the big lake not far down river.

Picking up two bats, he began loosening up his swing as Tracy, Gregory, Reginald, and several others from last year's squad emerged from the locker room to make their trips around the bases. When they finished, Coach Hanson called for squads to form up for calisthenics. As had been happening since the day on the pier, Reggie Billings took a place behind Jack and in tones inaudible to the coach but within earshot of the fellows nearby, resumed his taunting and teasing, making snide remarks about Jack's lack of courage.

Despite rising hostility, Jack made no reply, intent

instead on proving himself a good batsman against Reggie's fast balls and curves. When the jumping jacks and push-ups were over, he took his place in line with the other batsmen eager to try for the team.

The first hopeful at the plate, a sophomore, couldn't find the rhythm, swinging far too late at half a dozen pitches Reggie had placed precisely within the strike zone. The batsman finally made contact when Reggie slowed his pitch to half-speed. A ground ball hopped and skipped to left field where it was quickly snagged. The batsman next in line hit three balls foul down the first base line before connecting to slam a line drive past the player at shortstop.

Jack took his place in the batter's box, swung the bat twice, then nodded to Reggie in readiness. The first pitch, not a particularly fast ball, went outside. Jack let it go, surprised at Reggie's slowness and inaccuracy. The second pitch, a tad faster, flew inside. Again, Jack let it go, wondering if Reggie was having arm problems.

His concern was allayed by Reggie's next pitch, a perfect strike. It came over the plate so fast that Jack's swing was way too late. He watched Reggie close, wondering what he'd send next. A drop? A curve? A straight ball?

Reggie wound up and let the ball fly.

It went outside, then curved in and up, straight toward Jack's face!

He jumped back, landing on his rear!

Picking himself up, he glared at Reggie.

Billings smirked.

Ablaze with anger, Jack stomped toward the mound.

Coach Hanson followed.

"Weatherby, wait!"

Unmindful of all but inner fury, Jack planted himself squarely in front of Billings.

The pitcher's smile faded.

Quick as a flash, Jack sent two left jabs to his nose, then clobbered him with a right hook.

Reggie fell back, sprawled across the mound.

Finished with indoor chores, Isabelle went to the work shed late that afternoon intending to sort broom corn straw, but thoughts of Jack so distracted her, she could only sit on her stool and think. A vision of him hitting a baseball far into the outfield a week ago reminded her of how much she had enjoyed his company and how determined he was to earn a place on her brother's team.

"Dear Lord," she quietly prayed, "please be with Mr. Weatherby at practice today. You know how hard he's worked to win a position on the Erskine nine." Feelings of guilt stirring within, she added, "and forgive me for keeping my distance from him these last two days. He hasn't deserved such indifference on my part, but You know the reason for it."

As soon as the prayer left her lips, other thoughts took over. Picking up a recently completed pressed broom, she ran her thumb over the name on the handle, *T. Dorlon,* a name that hadn't changed in five generations of family broom making. She recalled, too, the words of her father—words he'd drilled into her from childhood.

"Customers buy our brooms because of the name on the handle. They know a *T. Dorlon* broom is the only broom worth having."

When she'd teased and begged to be allowed into the shed to watch her father work, he'd sent her off with a gruff reply. "In the Dorlon family, broom making is a *man's* job. Someday, your brother will be my apprentice and learn everything I know. Now, go on and tend to your studies so you can be a teacher when you grow up!"

And he never did let her inside the work shed—until he fell fatally ill and realized beyond all doubt that his children were bent on filling the roles he had chosen for them, but *in reverse.*

Setting the pressed broom aside, she glanced up at others hanging on the wall—cherished samples of the brooms her father had taught her to make—the colonial round broom, the hearth broom, the woven broom, the whisk broom, the curved broom. And always he had drilled into her the importance of the name on the handle. She could hear his words yet, weak with his dying breath.

"When I'm gone, tell our customers my son has taken over. They'll continue to buy as long as they know the brooms are made by one of the Dorlon men."

And so for the past two years she had carried on the ruse of making the brooms herself and applying the *T. Dorlon* name to the handles, telling store owners the work was that of her brother. She hated lying, but financial burdens had fallen heavy on the family since her father's demise and she couldn't risk losing good, steady customers. She could at least take solace in the fact that the quality of her work had measured up to that of her father, earning praise from shopkeepers who were always glad to see her.

Aside from high quality, another tradition she had kept up was that of letting no one outside the family enter the work shed. But unlike her father, who had simply claimed that he didn't want his sorted bundles of straw messed with, the practice had far more practical value. In this shed

48

where she came at night to work on her brooms while her beloved brother read aloud to her from his college texts and wrote out his class assignments, no one need ever discover the problem that for years had caused her no end of shame.

Her thoughts fled to Jack. How mortified she would be if he ever learned her secret. Reaching for a fistful of broom corn straw, she shoved the dreadful prospect from mind and attempted once again to concentrate on sorting. She had been at the task for only a few minutes when Chips came pawing at the shed door demanding her attention. Giving up on work for the time being, she went to fetch his leash from the kitchen, catching a delightful whiff of beef stew and a warning from her mother who was working biscuit dough into pea-sized crumbs.

"Don't stay away long. The boys will soon be here and I'll need your help getting dinner on the table."

"I'll be back in ten minutes," she promised.

When she returned, she set the table—minus one place since Anthony had been invited to the Jamisons—and helped her mother pour the stew into a serving dish. Little did she suspect that one hour later they would still be waiting for Tracy and his teammates to show up, wondering why no one had rung them up to explain the delay. Seconds after her mother had decided to start without the others, Isabelle heard the front door open.

Hurrying from the dining room, Tilda close behind, Isabelle encountered the most down-in-the-mouth assembly of ball players she'd ever seen—along with a stocky blond man she recognized as Coach Hanson.

Tracy spoke solemnly. "Mother, Coach Hanson would like a word with you."

"I'd like a word with him myself," she replied sharply.

To Hanson, she said, "I can't imagine why you would keep these fellows at practice an hour past dinner time."

"I'm truly sorry, Mrs. Dorlon. It's a complicated explanation. Can we sit and talk?"

"Come into the parlor," she said, indicating the door to his left.

Hanson instructed Tracy, Jack, and Gregory to join them, sending Reginald Billings upstairs instead.

When the pitcher stepped past Isabelle she saw that his cheek was cut and she assumed a fight had broken out. In the parlor, Jack was rubbing the knuckles of his right hand, his eyes downcast. Isabelle slipped into a chair near the door, her heart heavy with concern.

Coach Hanson fidgeted with the purple brim of his cap while he spoke.

"Mrs. Dorlon, Dean Levatt has expelled Reginald Billings from school for his behavior at practice today. He'll be leaving on the morning train."

Tilda replied instantly, "He's been in a fight, hasn't he?"

"It's a little more involved—"

She cut Hanson off, her gaze moving from Tracy to Jack to Gregory. "If any of the rest of you boys have been fighting, you'd better go upstairs and start packing, too. You know the rules. I won't tolerate hooligans or ruffians or brawlers in my home."

Jack shuffled his feet.

Isabelle shuddered, certain he was about to stand up and leave.

CHAPTER

6

A warning look from Coach Hanson kept Jack planted in his seat. Then the older man's explanation continued.

"Billings has had it in for Weatherby lately. Today, he pitched the ball right at Jack's head."

Isabelle gasped.

Jack addressed her mother forthrightly. "I was so angry I decked him one. I was wrong, but I just couldn't help myself."

Tilda scowled. "That's the second time in less than two weeks you've been in a fight, isn't it, Mr. Weatherby?

Tracy answered for him. "No, Mother, you're wrong. That time Jack got the cut lip, he was trying to *stop* a fight. *My* fight."

Tilda's eyes widened.

Gregory, who had been silent until now, began to confess also. "Billings and I . . . we said some things about Weatherby. Tracy took exception and started swinging at us. When Jack tried to break us up, he caught a blow meant for Tracy."

Tilda's visage darkened. "I'm deeply disappointed. Far as I'm concerned, the whole lot of you can pack your bags."

Tracy responded, "But Mother—"

She cut him off. "Tracy, you of all people, know how I

feel about fighting. I make no exception. Not even for my own son."

Coach Hanson spoke again. "Mrs. Dorlon, I don't blame you for the way you feel. You have every right to put these fellows out, but . . . won't you please reconsider?"

Tilda glowered. "Coach Hanson, are you defending such uncivilized behavior?"

"No, ma'am! All I'm saying is . . . it's only a few weeks to the end of the term. It would be mighty hard for them to find another place to live. Besides, we were counting on you for training table again this year, starting Thursday morning." He referred to the arrangement whereby the varsity team would take breakfast together each day at her table, thus enhancing her weekly income substantially during baseball season.

Silence ensued while Tilda pondered his words.

Isabelle prayed her mother would remember that the eaves needed cleaning, the porch needed painting, and the roof needed repair, and this was not the time to force her roomers from beneath it.

At last, Tilda revealed her decision. "All right, Coach Hanson, we'll play by *your* rules this time. Three strikes and you're out. But the very next time there's even a *hint* of a scuffle—"

He brightened. "There won't be. You have our word on it. Right, fellows?"

In chorus, they confirmed his promise.

He rose. Using his hat as a pointer, he addressed his players sternly. "From now on, I expect sterling behavior from you . . . and ten extra laps at every practice. I'll see you at four, sharp, tomorrow!"

Dinner was as solemn as it was late, Reginald taking his

meal in his room. Eight o'clock had come and gone by the time Isabelle went upstairs to fetch Billings' tray, Chips shadowing her in eager anticipation of the evening walk he'd been thus far denied. Knowing she couldn't put her faithful pet off any longer, she knocked on Jack's closed door.

"Come in," he replied.

She found him bent over books and papers on his desk, his glum expression brightening a tad when he saw her.

She spoke tentatively. "I probably shouldn't interrupt your studies. I know it's been a long day, but . . . could Chips and I impose on you for some company on our walk?"

On cue, the mutt brushed past her seeking Jack's favor with a wag of his tail and a lick on the bruised knuckles of his right hand.

He ruffled the dog's ear and smiled, secretly pleased by Isabelle's attention. Pulling on his sweater, he rose. "A walk is just what I need right now."

A few minutes later they were strolling through Monument Park, conversation almost nonexistent except for the one-way patter Isabelle kept up with Chips, praising him when he walked nicely beside her, admonishing him when he barked excessively at a stray cat. Jack was beginning to wonder if he had read more into the invitation than existed, considering the tension between them these last couple of days. Perhaps all she had wanted was the security of a male escort on her walk.

Isabelle glanced at Jack, his tall, athletic figure a comfort as she walked Chips on his after-dark tour. But she needed Jack tonight for more than the security of his company. She needed to share certain sentiments that were weighing heavily on her heart. Rounding the far corner of the square, they were approaching the bench where they had sat two days earlier when inspiration struck.

"Mr. Weatherby, would you please sit with me? There are some things I must say to you."

He grew suspicious. "Good things, I hope. I've had about all the dissension I can tolerate for one day."

Settling on the bench, she laughed. "No need to worry on that score."

He took a seat close beside her. When she gazed up at him, the lines and shadows of his face were handsome in the soft rays of the gas lamp. She enjoyed his nearness more than she'd realized, and distracting thoughts made her forget what she intended to say. She began anyway, trusting the Lord to supply her need.

"Mr. Weatherby—"

"Jack," he suggested.

"Jack." She tried his name softly, then continued as words of contrition came to her. "I shouldn't have walked off the way I did Sunday afternoon."

He opened his mouth to speak.

She raised a warning finger so near it almost touched Jack's lips, giving him the unexpected urge to kiss it.

He quelled the impulse and swallowed the words he'd wanted to say, listening instead to those of Isabelle.

"Worse than my walking away from you was my treating you with such indifference these last two days. Can you—will you—forgive me for all my offenses? . . . Please?"

Her eyes were filled with such hopefulness he wanted to reach out for her, draw her close, caress her. But their friendship was too tenuous for such affections.

He confined himself to a verbal response.

54

"Of course I forgive you."

His words played sweetly in her ear, until she heard his next sentence.

"On one provision, that is."

She shuddered to think what it might be. She would *not* answer questions about the work shed. When he continued, her fear proved unfounded.

"You must promise that if you're ever provoked with me in the future, you'll forego the silent treatment."

She smiled. "I promise!"

The wind gusted and Chips whined, straining impatiently on his leash.

Though words aplenty were swirling in Jack's head—words he longed to share with Isabelle—this was not the time.

He rose. "We'd better get back."

His hand at her elbow, he assisted her to her feet and kept her close beside him all the way home.

The mantle clock was striking nine when he helped her off with her wrap. Its bonging nearly drowned out the sound of someone knocking on the front door. Isabelle hurried to answer it, praying trouble had not come calling twice on the same day.

She was delighted to find a quartet of smiling faces on the other side of the door—Mr. and Mrs. Jamison along with Judith and Anthony. At the curb out front she recognized the silhouette of Mr. Jamison's Cadillac. The new automobile owner wasted no time revealing his reason for calling.

"Miss Isabelle, sorry to come unannounced. Could we please have a word with your mother?"

Mrs. Jamison jabbed him with her elbow. "Isabelle and Tracy, too, dear."

He amended his request. "And you and your brother, too."

"Come into the parlor." Isabelle showed them the way, then sought her mother in the kitchen where she was still putting away dinner dishes.

Tilda quickly untied her apron, wondering out loud, "What could possibly have brought the Jamisons here?"

"His new Cadillac, of course," Isabelle quipped.

"Of course. I shouldn't need reminding. It's all Anthony has talked about for days." She hung her apron on a peg and headed for the parlor while Isabelle rousted Tracy from his room upstairs.

When she and her brother joined the others, Mr. Jamison's enthusiastic chatter about his new motor car immediately gave way to the purpose for his unexpected visit.

"Mrs. Dorlon, as you probably know, Mr. Tidball, here, is going to River Bend in April for a big debate at Robinson."

"He's told me something to that effect," Tilda said wryly.

Mr. Jamison continued. "I'm personally quite interested in going over there to hear him. As it stands, my wife and I will be sailing for Detroit next week and can't make it. But Judith is going to River Bend—she'll be staying with close friends of ours—and she would be most appreciative if you'd allow Isabelle and Tracy to keep her company."

Anthony explained further. "Hardly anyone from Erskine will be there to support our debaters. You might be the only three in the audience on our side."

To Isabelle and Tracy, Judith said, "The two of you were so kind and helpful the day Jimmy fell in the river. Mother and Father want to do something in return."

Mrs. Jamison nodded. "We'll take care of the train passage. Once you arrive in River Bend, meals and accommodations will be seen to by our friends, the Shandlers."

Strengthening the argument, Anthony told Tracy, "My debate is on a Friday afternoon. The next day, Robinson plays a home ball game against Cartwright. It's your perfect opportunity to scout out the Robinson team—and the Cartwright team too, for that fact—see what you'll be up against."

Judith said, "Especially since your ball games that week are on Tuesday and Thursday rather than on the weekend, according to the schedule published in the *Centerport Daily.*"

Mrs. Dorlon focused on her son and daughter. "It's up to you. You're both old enough to decide whether or not you want to go."

Tracy turned to Isabelle. "I'd really like to go, but I won't go unless you want to."

Isabelle was torn. She'd never traveled as far as River Bend, only heard about it from Tracy after his ball games. This was her opportunity to see it firsthand—yet she was extremely hesitant to visit a city where she didn't know her way around, and even more reluctant to stay in an unfamiliar home with complete strangers. Still, she could hardly deprive Tracy of his chance to watch Robinson play ball. He deserved to go.

Speaking with enthusiasm she did not feel, she told Judith, "I'd love to go with you. Thank you for inviting me."

Jack awoke the following morning more tired than

57

when he'd gone to bed, it seemed. His run-in with Billings had replayed itself in a recurring nightmare. When he wasn't ducking to avoid a well-aimed baseball, he was listening to Coach Hanson read the roster for a varsity squad that did not include him in any position—not even substitute.

Contributing to his fatigue had been a very late bedtime hour following a lengthy discussion among Tracy, Anthony, Gregory, and himself about the upcoming trip to River Bend for the debate. It had rekindled a longing to visit his aunt and uncle, but he couldn't think about that now. Throwing back the covers, he washed and dressed. In the next room, he heard Billings slam shut the lid of his trunk. When Jack opened his door to head downstairs, Billings was right beside him.

"I'm gonna remember you, Weatherby," he said in a low, threatening tone. "I'm gonna remember you're the one who cost me my diploma from Erskine College."

Jack wanted to tell Billings it was his own fault, but he kept his silence, setting his books on the hall table, then taking his seat at breakfast.

As usual, Tilda Dorlon remained in the kitchen tending the eggs and bacon while Isabelle delivered them hot off the griddle. She set a steaming plate in front of Jack, and returned to the kitchen for more.

With the appearance of Billings, apprehension invaded the dining room. Evidently, no one seemed to know quite what to say to him. A tense silence ensued, broken by Billings whose words to Isabelle when she set his plate of eggs in front of him were enough to turn Jack's stomach.

"I'm gonna miss your bright, shining face, Isabelle. You're gonna miss me, too. Right?"

"I wish you well, Mr. Billings." Her quiet words rang with sincerity.

"Thank you, Isabelle." He caught hold of her wrist. "Now Reggie has some advice for you. Don't waste your time on cowards." His gaze burned into Jack.

Isabelle peeled Reggie's fingers from her wrist. "I don't know any cowards, Mr. Billings, except maybe you."

His face colored deeply. "Why, you—"

Tracy cut in. "Watch yourself, Billings."

"Watch myself? You'd better teach that sister of yours—"

Tilda Dorlon suddenly appeared, spatula jabbing the air. "Mr. Billings, you leave my house this instant, or I'll call on your former teammates to *put* you out!"

Tense seconds lapsed.

Tracy pushed back from the table.

Jack prayed it wouldn't come to blows.

CHAPTER

7

Reluctantly, Billings rose. "Don't bother to get up," he mumbled, "I know my way out of this dump."

Though tension subsided at the sound of him exiting the front door, Jack's appetite had taken leave. He somehow managed to finish his eggs and bacon before setting out for campus, but worries dogged his every step. He was oblivious to the sun shining brightly on his face, the greeting of robins from the elms in Monument Park, and the essence of Anthony's pipe tobacco as the debater preceded Jack across the square.

Once at school, the hours, like yesterday, crept by with maddening slowness. The irony of it set in when four o'clock finally approached and he could barely force his feet to carry him to the hall outside the locker room where the roster would be read.

Coach Hanson appeared on the dot of four, however, and the throng of hopefuls opened a path until he paused at the center of their midst, settling a pair of glasses on his nose and raising a slip of paper to read.

"The varsity roster is as follows. The regulars consist of Dorlon, Stiles, King, Knox, Gilberth . . . "

Jack held his breath. His heart pounding in his ears, he

strained to hear the remaining names.

"Motter, Bissell, Lowe, Northup. The substitutes are Smith, Griffin, Mears, and ... "

Jack prayed furiously during the momentary pause.

" ... Weatherby. You thirteen are to report to training table at Mrs. Dorlon's, eight o'clock tomorrow. Now, get into your baseball togs. We've got a lot of work to do."

Jack sent up a prayer of thanks. Though he'd missed the regular squad, he had enough experience to know anything could happen during the course of a season. A month from now, he might find himself one of the nine.

Two days later, on a Friday afternoon that found the players' bench bathed in unseasonably warm sunshine, Jack sat chin in hands watching Centerport High School go down to defeat in the first game of the varsity season. Though the score at the end of the sixth inning favored Erskine 9-0, not one of their runs had been earned, raising grave doubts in Jack's mind as to whether his much-coveted position on the team could ever qualify as the source of pride he had anticipated and strived for since boyhood.

When the regulars trotted out for the beginning of the seventh inning, he slid down the bench nearer Patterson, the manager, to glance at the score sheet. The error column was so filled with little black dots, it looked as though someone had sprinkled pepper on it. The outfielders had muffed every fly, quick recovery of the ball their only saving grace.

More errors accrued before the high schoolers were retired, then Erskine redeemed itself somewhat by piling up four more runs, two of them fairly earned.

Jack was resolved to spending the remainder of the

game on the bench when, at the start of the eighth inning, Hanson said, "Weatherby, replace Lowe in left field."

Hustling to his position near the rail fence, he suddenly caught sight of Isabelle in the crowd. She was sitting high up behind the Erskine bench, and he'd been unaware of her presence until now. His mission in the outfield took on a whole new meaning—not only to do well by his team, but to perform admirably in Isabelle's eyes. But opportunities to prove his prowess remained elusive when King, the pitcher, retired the opposing batsmen in one, two, three order. And his chance to show his skill with the stick went unfulfilled when a new pitcher for the opponents puzzled the batsmen so that only one reached first, and was left there at the start of the final inning.

From left field, Jack could see the bat boy packing away bats and onlookers beginning to leave the stands, including Isabelle. The opponents had reached the tail end of their batting list. To all appearances, the game was over.

He was surprised, therefore, when the first man at bat attempted to smash a long fly into the outfield. Instead, he wound up bunting the ball into the dust at his feet. Bewildered, he started for first, reaching it just prior to the ball.

High school supporters let out a fantastic war whoop. King, losing concentration, struck the next batsman on the elbow. Rubbing his bruise, he jogged to first while the man ahead took second.

Again, the game seemed over when King retired the next batsman in three pitches. But his successor at the plate connected with a straight ball, bunted toward first, and despite being tagged out, advanced runners to second and third. With the high schoolers' best batsman selecting his stick, a run seemed likely.

Hanson motioned the fielders in. Jack harbored doubts about the strategy, having observed the skill of the fellow at the plate. Making pretense of shortening field, he remained almost where he had been.

The lanky batsman stepped up to the plate. King delivered his pitch. The crack of ball against bat split the air.

Runners on third and second headed home. In the outfield, Bissell, center fielder, cut over into Jack's territory. Jack moved up field, fighting shadows to see the little black speck against the dusky sky.

Bissell, panting from his effort, cried, "All yours, Weatherby!"

Squinting, Jack stepped forward, put up his hands, and with a prayer, pulled the fly ball down. Catching a glimpse of Isabelle watching from behind the fence, he nearly dropped the ball, but managed to peg it to Perkins at second. A prayer of thanks on his lips, he trotted in, grateful that he had broken the outfield's string of errors.

Searching for his sweater at the bench, he looked up to find Isabelle lingering at the fence. She smiled and waved, then turned to go.

Moments later, he overheard Hanson telling Tracy, "At least we have one outfielder who can hold onto the ball."

In the locker room, Tracy clapped him on the back. "Great catch, Weatherby." The extent of his compliments evidently at an end, he proceeded to inform the team that he expected much better of them in the games to come, calling an extra practice to commence at eight in the morning.

Despite the prospect of a grueling workout, Jack kept the two positive comments in mind as he showered, dressed, and headed home, Tracy and Gregory walking silently alongside. But by the time he'd reached Elm

Street, reality had taken over, and he knew that any praise he'd earned today would prove small consolation for what portended to be a dismal season on the field.

Isabelle was in the kitchen mashing potatoes by the time the fellows came through the front door. She didn't have to see their faces to imagine the grim expressions pasted there. Familiar as she was with years of Tracy's first games, she passed off the season-starting disappointment as having little meaning regarding the rivalries to come. Smiling to herself, she pondered the plan she had already made to lift one sunken spirit in particular. When a somber dinner hour had ended, she climbed the stairs to propose it, finding the door to Jack's room open, its occupant gazing out the back window while a textbook lay ignored on the desk in front of him.

She knocked, letting herself in before invited. "That was a nice catch you made in today's game."

Jack swung around to face her. The gleam of her dark eyes, the glossiness of her mahogany hair, and the glow of her generous smile chased away gloomy thoughts of the upcoming season.

He smiled in return. "Thank you. It's kind of you to come all the way up here to tell me that."

"Actually, that's not all I had to say," she informed him. "We're having such a warm spell, I thought tomorrow would be a perfect day to picnic at the lagoon. The water should prove quite tepid."

His smile broadened. "A picnic sounds like the ideal way to recover from the workout Tracy has planned for us tomorrow morning."

"I'll have the picnic basket packed and the buckboard

hitched and ready when you get here," she assured him, returning to the kitchen to put the finishing touches on her chocolate cake.

Jack hustled hard throughout the Saturday morning practice, too exhausted when he arrived home to contemplate the prospect of a swimming lesson. But the opportunity to spend the afternoon with Isabelle was incentive enough to roll a pair of old cut-off pants into a towel and tuck them beside the picnic basket beneath the tarp on the buckboard, in the opposite corner from where Chips was perched.

When he climbed into the driver's seat beside Isabelle, she said, "I hope you don't mind Chips coming along. He loves the lagoon, and he hates being left behind."

Jack remembered his collie at home on the farm, and the way she had shadowed him until he went away to school. "I don't mind. You said he's a good swimmer. Maybe I'll learn something from him!"

They rolled down the drive and made their way to River Street, following it to the small deep water harbor a few blocks away. There, a freighter was unloading coal at the end of the main dock while a small steamer exchanged passengers for the next leg of its shoreline excursion.

Turning onto a narrow, tree-lined road, Isabelle drove another half mile or so before arriving at the edge of a pale aqua lagoon formed by a hundred-yard, manmade inlet from the big lake. Sand dunes overlooked the pond from behind, guarding waters both placid and inviting, unlike the chop on the bluer surface beyond where gulls glided and soared, cried and plunged, holding a picnic of their own.

Chips was the first one out, bounding to the lagoon, stepping cautiously into the water. Finding it to his liking, he swam enthusiastically in a circle before bounding onto dry sand to shake himself. A heavy spray of water rained over Isabelle and Jack as he helped her down from the buckboard.

She turned her back to the unavoidable shower and laughed. "Chips, you rascal! You could at least have waited till we got our bathing suits on!" To Jack, she said, "If you'll help me with the tarp, we can put up a makeshift dressing room for changing."

He held it up while she pinned it to three closely spaced saplings. Then he waited for her to change before undressing to his undershirt and putting on his cut-off pants. He was reluctant to emerge from behind the tarp attired so. Not only was he embarrassed about his lack of a proper bathing costume, but also about the revealing nature of his outfit.

By comparison, Isabelle had put on a navy blue flannelette suit trimmed in rows of white braiding on the collar and sleeves, its below-the-knee skirt revealing legs clad in stockings with soles. It was the latest in bathing fashions, he was certain.

Stepping out from behind the tarp, he felt compelled to explain. "I don't have a bathing suit. I hope these will do."

She grinned. "You and Tracy. What is it about Erskine baseball players? He doesn't wear a proper bathing suit when he comes here, either!"

Led by Chips to the edge of the lagoon, she tested the water with her toes while he marched right in and swam away. Though Jack watched with the semblance of a smile, she read the apprehension in his countenance, then tried to allay his fears.

"The water's warmer than usual for this time of year. If

you come in slowly and give yourself a chance to get used to it, you'll be all right."

He followed her in, every fiber of his being resisting the process. Over a few minutes' span, he'd gone deep enough for the water to envelope his ankles and knees.

Sensing Jack's hesitance, Isabelle resolved to tease it away. When she was in waist deep, she sent him a splash that sprinkled his shirt. He flinched.

"It's not that bad, is it?" she asked with a grin.

Conceding nothing, he stepped toward her, cupped both hands, then sent a healthy spray of water against her upper body.

"Now, you've done it!" she warned, plunging in and kicking hard as she swam away.

Thoroughly dampened by her splashing, Jack had no excuse but his own fear to prevent him from descending deeper. Forcing nightmarish memories from his mind, he took one reluctant step after another until water covered his thighs and circled his waist. There, he came to a standstill.

She must have noticed, for she soon returned. "You're making progress, Mr. Weatherby! Now I have an idea."

"Jack," he reminded her, petrified that she would ask him to walk in up to his neck.

"Jack," she repeated.

Moving a little closer to shore, she lowered herself in the clear water, her skirt floating out around her. "When I was little, I was afraid to let the water come up past my waist. Then Tracy taught me to sit on the bottom. I *felt* like I was in up to my neck, but I *knew* the water wasn't even waist-deep."

Jack bent his knees, allowing the pond to rise around

him a few inches, then stood up again.

Seeing his willingness, yet sensing his need to face this challenge on his own terms, Isabelle eased away. "I'll be back in a few minutes."

Thankful for time alone, he watched her stroke to the opposite shore. As she frolicked with Chips in the sand, she often glanced his way to check on his progress. But he was unable to make himself sit on the bottom. Defeated by fear, he prayed.

"Lord, please give me the strength and courage to do as Isabelle suggested."

He began to lower himself again. After three more attempts, he managed to plant his backside on the sandy bottom. Isabelle was soon beside him once more.

"Very good, Jack! Now for the next step. Can you put your face in the water?"

He'd done that as a child in the bath tub—until the incident at the farm pond.

"I . . . don't know," he admitted with reluctance.

Putting her chin and mouth in the water, Isabelle began to blow bubbles.

The sound made Jack chuckle. A few minutes later, he was blowing bubbles, too.

Next, Isabelle encouraged him to put his entire face in the water, including nose and eyes. Though she demonstrated the simple act in many ways—holding her nose, without holding her nose, plunging her entire head beneath the surface, and leaning back until water rippled over her face—Jack could not seem to take the next step.

Concluding that further progress would have to wait until another day, Isabelle decided to ask Jack simple questions about himself, convinced that the longer he stayed in the pond, the more comfortable he would become with the feel of water surrounding him. Her inquiries would serve other purposes, too. She was truly interested to discover his past, a subject he'd shared but little, except for his involvement with baseball. And if she could get him to reveal the reason for his fear of water, she would be better able to help him overcome it.

Jack was unaccustomed to talking about himself and his family, but he tried to answer Isabelle's questions about his folks, whom she had met briefly on the day he'd moved into the Dorlon home a few months earlier. At her prompting, he spoke also of his life on their family farm, then he turned the tables and asked her to describe her late father.

A dark look graced her brow before she pasted on a half-smile. "He was the hardest-working man I've ever known."

Before Jack could draw her out on the topic, she rattled on at length about her childhood in Centerport, and how she and Tracy had loved spending their mornings watching the steamers at the harbor, their afternoons swimming in the lagoon, and their evenings at a vacant lot on Balcom Street where Tracy and his friends would play baseball. From this lengthy discourse of her youth, she switched abruptly to another question about Jack's farm days.

"Did you have a dog to help with your cows? I sometimes think Chips would be good at bringing cows in for milking." Her own mention of her beloved dog provoked lines of worry. "I just realized I haven't seen hide nor hair of Chips in quite a while." She scanned the perimeter of the lagoon, her gaze coming to rest on the sandy hill at their backs.

There, loose sand was flying in spurts over the crest of

the dune.

"Chips! Where are you, boy?"

The yellow dog's head popped up above the dune, his pointed ears held erect.

She grinned. "There you are! Now, go back to your digging. Better here, than in the back yard."

No sooner had she spoken than he did as she said, sand sailing by the pawfuls, sending both Isabelle and Jack into laughter.

When the moment had passed, she focused on Jack again. "You were going to tell me about *your* dog. Then I want to know what you did for a pastime—besides baseball, that is—and tell me the funniest thing that ever happened to you while you were growing up."

By the time Jack had described his collie, Kella, who had been a kleptomaniac in her youth, pilfering slippers, socks, and mittens, he found himself completely comfortable sharing memories of his childhood. Perhaps the reason was Isabelle's own talkative nature. Every anecdote he told of life on his family farm was matched or exceeded by Isabelle's remembrances of growing up near the big lake.

He spoke at length about himself in a way he'd never done before, telling of the six years he attended school in River Bend. Describing his aunt, uncle, and cousins—Catherine who was two years older and Clifford who was his same age and was attending school out East—he explained that they had been like a second family to him.

Isabelle proved the most avid listener and skilled conversationalist he'd ever encountered. He couldn't help feeling flattered by her attention and her keen interest, especially in the city she would soon visit.

70

He therefore found it easy to reply when she asked him to describe the scariest incident he could remember.

"That would be the day I fell into the pond on the farm," he said frankly.

Anxious to learn details, Isabelle again couldn't stem her flow of questions. "How old were you? How did it happen? Were you alone?" Her velvet brown eyes focused on him intently.

He surprised himself with the ease of his response. "I was five years old, kneeling at the edge of the water, trying to catch tadpoles. I leaned too far. The pond was spring-fed and frigid, and way over my head."

"You probably thought you were going to die!"

Jack nodded. "And I would have if Mama hadn't been watching me from the barnyard. She came running and hauled me out by the collar. I hardly remember that part, though."

"Did you swallow a lot of water?"

Again, he nodded. "I coughed until my belly hurt. But that wasn't the worst of it. For years afterward, I had terrifying nightmares."

"And in every nightmare you were falling into a freezing cold pond and struggling to catch your breath. No wonder you never learned to swim." She reached for Jack's hand, squeezing it. "But that's going to change."

He squeezed her hand in return, certain she was right. Then he rose and pulled her to her feet. "It's time we got dried off and changed."

"And ate some lunch. I'm hungry!" Isabelle admitted without compunction.

When they arrived onshore, Jack said, "You change first. Then you can spread lunch while I get dressed. But

71

would you please toss me my towel so I can dry off?"

She nodded, approaching the makeshift dressing room. But the instant she stepped inside, she realized that while they were bathing, a visitor had come to call. Not only were her own towel and togs missing, but also Jack's. She flung back the tarp.

"Our clothes are gone!"

Gazing about, Jack's focus settled on the buckboard. The picnic basket was no longer in the corner, where they'd left it, but had been shifted to the center. Lifting the lid, he exclaimed, "Our lunch is missing, too!"

As if one, they focused on the sand dune and cried out in unison.

"Chips!"

Their call elicited no response.

Isabelle strode up the hill, grumbling to Jack as she went. "When I find that mutt, I'm going to—"

He finished for her. "—give him a tongue lashing like he's never heard before."

Too angry to reply, she trekked to the top of the hill in silence, appalled at the scene that lay just beyond the crest.

Half-buried in the sand were her towel, skirt, and blouse. Strewn on the ground were Jack's towel, shirt, and pants, each showing evidence of Chips's teeth.

Nearby were empty paper wrappers, depleted of all but a few crumbs of the ham sandwiches and chocolate cake she had so carefully prepared. Most pathetic of all was the look on the dog's face as he lay on his side, belly bloated, an empty container of potato salad a few inches from his snout.

Isabelle knelt beside him. "You look like you're going to be sick, and it serves you right." He licked her hand, emitting such a pitiful whine, her anger dissipated. She took him gently by the collar. "Get up, boy. We're going home. And I hope we get there before your lunch comes back to haunt you."

While she led the culprit to the buckboard, Jack collected and shook out the towels and clothing. Then he took down the tarp and put everything on the bed of the buckboard including Chips, who now seemed incapable of jumping up under his own power.

Isabelle took reins in hand and started down the rutted road. "I'm sorry Chips was so naughty today. I'll replace your shirt and pants."

"Don't worry. Remember what I said about Kella? Dogs seem to go through a filching stage when they're young and playful." He glanced back to check on the sick mutt, who had risen to his feet and was starting to heave. "You'd better pull over. Your pup is about to lose his lunch."

Jack leaped down, lifting Chips from the buckboard and setting him on the ground just in time. Moments later, he had recovered sufficiently to climb onto the bed of the buckboard under his own power.

Isabelle started for home again, more slowly than before. She was apologizing the second time for her dog's mischievousness when he started to growl. Before she could find the reason, he leaped off the buckboard, barking frantically as he ran down the road.

Then she saw his intended prey. A bushy black rodent with a wide white stripe down her back!

73

CHAPTER

8

Isabelle perched on her stool facing the west wall of the work shed, Chips at her feet. As she stared at the placards tacked to the boards in front of her, she tried to ignore the fact that her mutt still smelled slightly from his encounter with the skunk five days ago and concentrate instead on her self-imposed morning lesson.

Starting at the upper left corner of the wall, she began to recite out loud. "Vowels—a, e, i, o, u, y. Consonants—b, c, d, f, g . . . "

On she went until she had reviewed all the letters of the alphabet, a score of diphthongs, and a dozen simple words and phrases Tracy had written out and posted for her. But the sounds seemed meaningless. The curse of her inability to read despite years of trying was back to haunt her full force now that the trip to River Bend loomed on tomorrow's horizon. She couldn't bear the thought that the Shandlers might discover her dark secret, or the other problems she suffered along with her inability to learn.

Studying the placards again, she thanked God that her brother had never given up on her. She recalled her first year in grammar school. Unable to memorize the alphabet, read simple words, or understand easy arithmetic problems, she had grown frustrated, anxious, and naughty. When her grammar school teacher had told her mother not to send her to school again until she had learned to read and cipher, Tracy had taken it upon himself to read to her from his texts when completing his homework each night. When she had been unable to tell right from left, he was the one who suggested tying the colored ribbon on her right wrist. And when she had been unable to tell time from a clock, he explained the movement of the hands in a dozen different ways until she finally caught on.

But many problems remained for which Tracy had found no answers. At times she would forget what she was doing in the few seconds it took her to walk from one room to the next. She became easily confused and disoriented inside unfamiliar buildings. And when fretful, she bumped into things—including furniture that hadn't been recently moved.

Reciting the information on the placards once more, she attempted to grasp the words and phrases posted in front of her. But not only could she make no sense of them, she couldn't seem to control her rising panic over tomorrow's trip to River Bend.

On the edge of tears, she fled to the house, bursting through the back door.

"Mama!"

When Tilda didn't answer, Isabelle called again, her voice shrill with anxiety.

"Mama! Where are you?"

Faintly came the reply. "I'm in the fruit cellar, dear."

Isabelle flew down the basement steps, bumping into an old chair and upsetting a stack of dented pots which clattered to the floor.

Her mother was emerging from the storage room, her arms laden with quart jars of fruits and vegetables, when

Isabelle ran into her. Only Tilda's quick reflexes prevented the Ball jars from hitting the floor and shattering.

She scolded mildly. "Careful, girl. What is it?"

"I can't go tomorrow! I *can't!*"

Tilda spoke soothingly. "Calm yourself, child."

Too distraught to pay heed, Isabelle carried on.

"Mama, I'll make a fool of myself! I'll be a laughing-stock! All of River Bend will think I'm a simpleton!"

Her mother remained calm. "Let's go upstairs, make ourselves some tea, and talk."

A few minutes later Isabelle and her mother settled on the love seat in the parlor and sipped Darjeeling from the good china cups usually reserved for company. Morning sunshine streamed through the windows casting rectangles of light on the burgundy carpet and brightening the ivory walls with the promise of a perfect spring day. But inside, Isabelle sensed darkness overtaking her.

She set her cup on the tray with a clunk. "I wish I'd never said I'd go tomorrow. I'm going to ring up Judith and tell her I'm sick." Before she could rise, her mother laid a staying hand on her arm.

"Just what is so troublesome about going to River Bend that would make you tell an outright lie?"

"Everything!" Isabelle insisted. "Just . . . everything! Meeting strange people, staying in a strange house, going about in a strange city."

"Tracy will be with you."

"I know. But if the Shandlers are like the Jamisons, they have a big house with lots of rooms. I probably won't be able to go from their parlor to the guest bedroom without getting lost or running into things. And I'm a complete failure at small talk!"

Tilda set aside her tea, taking Isabelle's hands in hers. "Dear, you worry too much. Tracy and Judith will help you find your way around the Shandlers' place. And we'll practice the art of polite conversation right now, if you like."

Tears of frustration sprang to Isabelle's eyes. Pulling free of her mother's touch, she took to the front stairs, her words trailing behind her. "It's no good, Mama! I'm not going!"

In the sanctuary of her room, she flopped on her bed and sobbed. "Why, Lord? *Why* can't I learn? Why can't I comprehend the simplest things?"

She cried so hard, her bed shook. The tears streaming down her face flowed rich with pent-up frustration over years of failure. Humiliation and shame would surely bedim her future.

Chips, evidently hearing her weep, came to lick the tears from her cheeks, but his affection was of little consolation. A while later, weary, she welcomed her mother's tap on the door, and the company she offered as she seated herself on the edge of Isabelle's bed.

Offering a clean handkerchief and gentle hug, Tilda spoke with great affection. "I love you just as you are, Isabelle. I hope you know that."

"Yes, Mama. I do."

Brushing Isabelle's cheek with her hand, Tilda continued. "It pains me to see you suffer, child. I've prayed hundreds—no, thousands of times that you would get over your reading trouble, but that's one prayer the Lord hasn't seen fit to answer yet."

Isabelle had prayed, too. First, as a child, that God would let her learn like other children. And now, as a young woman, that maturity would make a difference. But it seemed as if those prayers were a waste.

Her mother continued. "I'm going to tell you something I've never told you before. It's about your father."

Isabelle squeezed her eyes shut and turned away. Her relationship with her father had been difficult, and except for the last year of his life, distant. Only when he understood the gravity of his illness and the fact that his daughter was his last hope for the survival of the Dorlon broom making business, did she spend extended periods of time in his company.

But the hours were never easy. With great difficulty she managed to learn his craft—at the price of much bickering, frustration, and strain. His praise had been tightly rationed, coming primarily at the end of his days when she had mastered all the skills to create top quality brooms. Even then he continued to express regrets that it would be his daughter, not his son, who would carry on. But with a look, a word, a touch, he told her he loved and respected her, and she had loved him, too, her feelings growing stronger as his strength began to slip away.

With memories such as these, Isabelle had no desire to dwell on the past, but her mother proceeded to share what was on her mind.

"When your papa was a child, he had the same trouble with schooling that you did. He couldn't read or cipher."

The words cut through the cloud of sadness shrouding Isabelle's memories. She sat up, suddenly attentive. "But he learned later."

Her mother shook her head. "He went to his death bed unable to read more than the headline of the morning paper."

"But he read from the Bible," Isabelle argued, "and the hymn books at church. And when Tracy and I were real little, he read stories to us."

"It was all from memory," her mother explained. "He couldn't read the words. And he left all the ciphering to me. Did you ever see him add up a column of figures?"

Isabelle thought a moment. "At Reilly's General Merchandise, when Mr. Reilly would write down all the amounts on the brown paper and add them up, Papa could do it upside down and tell if it was right."

"No, dear. It was I who added them upside down and passed a signal to your papa if Mr. Reilly had made a mistake."

For a minute or more Isabelle was awestruck by the knowledge, scrambling to comprehend the basic truth that her father had been as troubled by words and numbers as she was. "I'm just like him," she thought out loud. "I'm just like him, but I never knew it . . . till now. Why didn't he tell me?"

"He had his dignity," her mother replied. Then, with a quiver in her voice, she added, "He had his dignity, and for as long as he was alive, that was more important to him than the truth."

Sympathy dueled with anger as Isabelle absorbed the fact. "But all these years I thought it was just me. That I was the only one in the world with this trouble."

A tear spilled down her mother's cheek. "I'm sorry, child. I wanted to tell you, but I . . . " Her voice choked with sobs.

Isabelle embraced her mother, the two of them crying quietly for a time. When their tears subsided, her mother again took hold of her hands.

"Isabelle, dear, I can understand your worry about visiting the Shandlers, but it's best to accept your shortcomings and move on. Otherwise, you're going to cheat yourself out of life."

Isabelle's puzzlement must have shown on her face, for her mother offered further explanation.

"You've struggled for years—since you were six—to learn how to read. The Lord just hasn't seen fit to give you that gift. If you explain it that way to others, they won't judge you harshly."

Struggling to comprehend her mother's wisdom, Isabelle asked, "Do you mean I should . . . quit trying to read?"

"No. I mean you should quit being ashamed because you can't."

She pondered the concept. "But what if I admit to someone I can't read, and he—I mean she—decides not to have anything to do with me. You know how it was when I went to school." Memories of cruel remarks and shunning from classmates had taught her early to put up a tight guard concerning her inadequacies.

Her mother regarded her with sympathy. "You're worried about what Mr. Weatherby would think if he knew you couldn't read, aren't you?"

Isabelle hung her head.

"Here's what I think. If he can't like you as you are, then he's not worthy of your friendship."

The words, *Easy for you to say,* ran through Isabelle's mind.

Her mother continued. "But I think Mr. Weatherby is more understanding, and more fond of you than to let your reading problem come between you."

Isabelle's gaze met her mother's. "I still don't want him to know."

A thoughtful moment passed before her mother replied. "You could explain it to Jack this way. Some people, like your brother, are given a talent for reading, writing, and baseball, but when it comes to painting the front porch, the place looks worse after he's finished than when he started. Others are given a talent for making brooms, but can't seem to understand the fine print on the page of a newspaper."

When Isabelle remained silent, her mother said, "Just promise me this—when you've found someone special enough to spend the rest of your life with, you'll tell him about your reading problem before you walk down the aisle." Growing reflective, she added, "It's downright unfair to be deceitful about something as . . . as significant as reading."

Isabelle contemplated the implication. "You mean you didn't know Papa couldn't read when you married him?"

Her mother shook her head. "I would have married him anyway, I loved him so much. But he could have saved me a passel of misunderstanding and heartache in the first few years if he'd only been honest from the start."

The words gave Isabelle pause. She was still contemplating them moments later when the downstairs clock struck ten and her mother rose. "How time flies. I've got to get to market if I'm going to cook pot roast for dinner. You'd better see to some packing while I'm gone."

Isabelle lay down again, unable to work up enthusiasm for the trip, for the household chores needing attention, or even for the afternoon game against Oakwood that she had been planning to attend. She heard her mother ring up someone on the phone—presumably the butcher to place her order for the pot roast—then head out the front door. Drifting into a light sleep troubled by worries over the impending sojourn, Isabelle was soon awakened by the ringing of the doorbell.

Tucking an errant strand of hair into the twist at the back of her head, she hurried to answer the front door, finding Judith on the doorstep.

Her friend greeted her enthusiastically. "Sorry to arrive unannounced. I was in the neighborhood and thought I'd stop by to see if I could help with packing for our trip to River Bend tomorrow."

"I . . ." Isabelle tried to tell Judith she wouldn't be going, but when the words wouldn't come, she said simply, "I could use some help."

Waving off her driver, Judith stepped inside, deposited her hat and gloves on the hall table, and took the lead up the stairs. In the next hour, she helped Isabelle choose and pack the appropriate outfits for the weekend's itinerary, all the while telling about the Shandlers and their home.

Judith seemed to understand without being told that the problems Isabelle had suffered during her earliest school days were plaguing her still. She described everything about their upcoming trip several times, pausing afterward to make sure Isabelle understood and to give her an opportunity to repeat the information. In detail, Isabelle recited the layout of the first floor with its guest wing, the most popular topics for conversation among the various members of the Shandler family, and even the riddles young Sheridan Shandler was fond of for stumping house guests.

When they had finished, Judith accepted Isabelle and her mother's invitation to stay to lunch, complimenting the corned beef sandwiches and dessert of canned pears more highly than such simple fare deserved. She revealed, too, a special arrangement her father had made to ensure pleasant travel and meals during the train trip. When her driver returned to fetch her at one o'clock, she parted with the reminder that they would come calling to collect Isabelle, Tracy, and their bags at eleven the following morning.

Her worries transformed to anticipation regarding River Bend, Isabelle adjourned to the work shed planning to fashion at least one broom before quitting to attend the baseball game. The sight of the sample brooms made and hung by her father aroused feelings she had never felt before. Knowing how deeply her own father had suffered from the inability to read brought a sense of profound sympathy and love. The two of them had been alike in more ways than she had ever imagined and she regretted deeply that he had been unable to own up to his shortcomings before his death.

She continued to mull over these thoughts as she completed a pressed broom. Then, she set her work room in order with needles, waxed string, and leather palm neatly in their place. Pausing at the door, she stared one more time at the brooms created by her father's hands. They held a new meaning for her now, causing her to cherish them in a way she never had before. Taking Erskine pennant in hand, she slowly closed the door behind her, then set a brisk pace to the college ball field to see the game against Oakwood.

Remaining benched during the first seven innings of the game, Jack had ample time to locate Isabelle in the stands. He'd had plenty of opportunity to study the clouds rolling in off the big lake and thickening over the ball field, as well. With the smell of rain in the air and the sound of thunder in the distance, he prayed the storm would hold off long enough to finish the game.

Now, at the top of the eighth inning, the score stood at three apiece with a man on third, no outs, and the star Oakwood batsman at the plate. Jack had given up the possibility of seeing action during the last two innings when the Oakwood man hit a line drive into left field. The runner on third scored easily while the batsman rounded first, then slid safely into second, colliding heavily with Perkins and knocking him to the ground. Perkins pulled himself up, tested his left ankle, and unable to walk on it, sought Bissell and Knox to assist him to the bench.

Hanson turned to Jack. "Weatherby, cover second."

He sprinted to his assignment, praying for a good arm and steady hands should the ball come his way. But the position worried him. He had virtually no experience there.

He studied the next batsman, a leftie. From the way he swung, Jack was certain he would hit hard into right field if he connected with the ball. King, the replacement pitcher following Billings' expulsion, was getting tired. He had difficulty finding the strike zone, reaching a count of 0 and 3 before sending a pitch over the plate.

The batsman swung and hit. A ground ball leaped past King. Jack stooped. The ball hopped. Over his glove and between his feet it rolled.

Bissell, the center fielder, snagged it and pegged it to Tracy at first. Too late to make the out, Tracy threw home, holding the runner at third.

Humiliated by his error, Jack resolved to keep his feet together in the future.

The next batsman hit a fly ball that was caught foul of the third base line. With another man up, the runner at first took an extraordinarily big lead. The first pitch resulted in a grounder going to the shortstop. He threw to first. The throw went wild. By the time Tracy recovered it, runners were advancing to second and third. Tracy threw to Jack. The ball hit the edge of his glove and sailed on. By the time he had retrieved it and sent it home, the score stood five to three with a man on third and one out.

Jack knew he should have caught Tracy's throw. It had been accurate enough, but in the heat of the moment, Jack had taken his eye off it. Bereft of confidence, Jack prayed the ball would head anywhere but to second. The inning ended with two successive strikeouts.

With Erskine at bat, Jack's opportunity to show his skill came with two outs and Tracy on first. He stepped up to the plate and swung the bat twice, then stood ready for the first pitch, muscles tense, nerves taut.

The pitcher wound up and let fly with a fast ball. Jack tried to calculate its speed, but it hit the catcher's mitt before he'd even completed his swing.

Realizing his timing was off—way off—he was determined to anticipate the next pitch. Squeezing the bat tightly, he studied the man on the mound. When the ball left his hand, Jack swung.

CHAPTER

9

Jack's swing was late, but this time he connected, hitting high down the first base line. On a direct path with the pole, the ball deflected into the stands—a home run! Cheers and applause sent him on his trip around the bases, renewing his confidence.

But as he rounded first, another kind of applause spurred him on—a loud clap of thunder. Sprinkles dampened his face as he headed toward third. Then a bolt of lightning split a large black cloud above the stands releasing torrents of rain. Fans and players alike ran for cover.

Disappointed by the timing of the heavenly deluge, Jack gathered his sweater and glove from the bench and sprinted for the locker room. As he stood in the shower letting the spray pelt down across his shoulders, he took solace in the fact that he had been able to bring Tracy in and tie up the score at five apiece. The game had not gone down as a loss on the Erskine record.

Equally important, he thought, *At least I redeemed myself in the eyes of Isabelle and my teammates.*

The words gave him pause.

He mentally reviewed them, astonished not by their content, but by their order. Without realizing it, he had begun placing Isabelle's opinion of him above that of his teammates.

By the time Isabelle arrived home from the game she was soaked to the skin, requiring a complete change of clothing before helping her mother serve the pot roast. But the rain, which gave way to sunshine minutes after she reached the house, hadn't dampened her newfound anticipation of the trip to River Bend. After dinner, in the work shed with Tracy, she could sense his excitement, too. When he had opened his text to study for an early morning exam on British writers, the words he spoke were not those read from the page before him, but of travel plans.

"Don't you worry about tomorrow. I'll be with you every minute to make sure nothing goes wrong. And if a situation comes up where someone expects you to read—"

"I'll say I haven't been given that gift," Isabelle quietly interrupted.

Tracy cocked his head. "Beg your pardon?"

She repeated the words more confidently. "I'll say I haven't been given that gift."

"But—"

"Mama and I had a talk this morning. She says it's best to be honest, and she's right. There's something else she said, too." Isabelle paused, framing her disclosure as a question. "Tracy, did you know Papa couldn't read?"

His visage darkened. "Mama told you that?"

Isabelle nodded. "He couldn't do arithmetic, either."

His color rising, Tracy paced the floor. Pausing by the broom handles Isabelle had propped neatly in the corner for future use, he studied them a moment. Suddenly, without warning, he grabbed one and began swinging, knocking down the brooms his father had made and hung on the wall as examples for Isabelle.

"Tracy, stop!" she cried.

He paid no heed, bashing and batting at the fallen samples.

Splinters flying, Isabelle shrank back against the opposite wall.

"Stop! Please!" she pleaded again, shielding herself with upraised arms from flying wood chips and broom corn. Outside, she could hear Chips barking, growling, and scratching the door.

Moments later, fury spent, Tracy dropped what was left of the broom handle he'd been wielding and slumped onto his stool.

Assessing the damage, Isabelle knelt to retrieve the fragments of her father's fancily-woven, curved-handled whisk broom, tears springing to her eyes as she gingerly lifted it from the clutter-strewn floor and feebly attempted to tuck stray stems of broom corn back into place.

Clearly regretful of the upset he had caused, Tracy knelt beside her, his hand tender on her shoulder. "Isabelle, I'm sorry. I didn't mean—"

"Leave me alone!" she warned, shrugging off his touch.

"I didn't mean to distress you," he quietly insisted. "I'll clean this up." Springing to his feet, he grabbed the pressed broom Isabelle had completed earlier and began sweeping with a vengeance.

"Tracy, stop!" she commanded.

Her shrill words made him freeze. She rose to face him, confusion and disappointment bubbling up inside.

"Tracy, what on earth were you doing? What made you so angry?"

He hung his head. "I . . . I'm not sure."

"You've *got* to learn better control of your temper."

"I know . . . I know." His gaze rose to meet Isabelle's. "I suppose when you told me Papa couldn't read, it made me mad that he pretended to know how all those years."

She bent to retrieve another piece of her father's handiwork—a portion of a particularly pretty broom handle that had been cut from a walnut tree, a tiny face carved into the polished knob at the top. It was the last carving he'd done before his blood disease had made him too sick to come to the work shed.

"You know," she said contemplatively, "making brooms is the one thing Papa and I could do as well as—or even better than—people who know how to read. It's the good side of his legacy to me, and now, the last of his handiwork is . . . " She choked up. Tears trickling down her cheeks, she turned away.

Tracy came beside her, offering his handkerchief. "I'm sorry, Isabelle, *so* sorry. I never meant to hurt you. Please forgive me."

Isabelle took the handkerchief he offered—one she'd embroidered with his initials and given him on his birthday last year. It reminded her of similar ones she'd given her papa, handkerchieves Tracy had refused to use after their father had died. Memories of the strife between father and son that had lasted right up to the end brought a new insight to Isabelle.

She dabbed her cheeks. "You know what I think, Tracy? I think you're upset because you never made peace with Papa. You let anger come between you until he went to his grave, then it was too late."

Pensive, Tracy began to calmly sweep clutter into a

small pile. Pausing to lean against the broom, he told Isabelle, "I suppose you're right, but if I were to be perfectly honest, that's only part of it."

Isabelle remained silent, hoping he'd continue as she stooped to collect more remnants of her father's carvings. A minute later, her brother spoke again.

"If Papa couldn't read, and you can't read, then he must have passed the curse on to you. It makes me angry, knowing how much you've suffered over the years because of it."

She contemplated his words while clearing a place on her work table for the splintered wood she'd salvaged. Moments later, Tracy came to her with a broken piece of broom handle. Holding it at eye level, he revealed the name, *T. Dorlon,* which had been tapped into its surface.

"Isabelle, if you're going be honest with people about the fact that you can't read, then it's time you start being honest about who is really making the brooms in this work shed. From now on, you put *I.* Dorlon on each one."

When she made no reply, he said, "Promise me you'll do it."

Assessing the ramifications of his request, she reluctantly replied, "All right. I suppose it makes no difference if I lose my customers, now that your schooling is paid for."

"You won't lose your customers. I doubt they'll even notice."

"They'll notice," she assured him.

"Then you'll have to tell them what you should have told them in the first place. That it's been *you* making the brooms since Papa died, not me."

Isabelle couldn't argue, but as she resumed her search for salvageable remnants of her father's work, she couldn't help praying that her broom making business wouldn't come to an abrupt end.

Nothing further was said until Tracy had finished sweeping up and sat down to review his English Literature in preparation for his morning exam. The sound of his voice reading to Isabelle while she worked at her bench restored the old, familiar sense of sibling harmony—except for the fact that her hands were occupied by the task of repairing an old, cherished broom rather than the routine of creating a new one.

Much later, when Tracy had finished his review of Sir Thomas Malory's Arthurian cycle and he and Isabelle were ready to call it a night, he paused, his hand on the door handle.

"Isabelle, I truly am sorry for the damage I did. I promise to keep my temper under control during the trip to River Bend."

Solemnly, she warned, "You had better!" With a hint of a smile and a shake of a finger, she added, "You'd better promise me you'll come directly home after your exam tomorrow, too. Judith will be collecting us at eleven for the ride to the depot."

Tracy grinned as he opened the door for her. "That's an easy promise to keep."

Outside, Isabelle noticed that Jack was sitting on the back porch steps. Chips, who had settled beside him to beg for affection, bounded to his mistress the moment he saw her.

Jack came down off the steps, his comment directed at Isabelle as she and Tracy approached him. "Your dog has been waiting patiently for his walk. I know it's late, but I'll be glad to come along if you still want to take him."

Tracy jabbed a friendly elbow into his teammate's ribs. "Don't keep my sister out long, Weatherby. She's got a big weekend coming up."

Isabelle kept her silence as her brother disappeared inside the house, then reached down to ruffle her pet's ear. "Do you want to go for a walk, boy?"

He barked in eagerness, his tail thumping against her skirt with each sweeping wag.

To Jack, she said, "Chips and I accept your offer! I'll fetch his leash."

They hadn't walked far when Jack initiated conversation. "I heard some loud noises when you were working in the shed. Is everything all right?"

Isabelle paused. In the fringe of the street light she detected a crease over Jack's brow that contradicted the casual tone of his question. The urge to reveal the truth of dark family secrets and her troubling encounter with Tracy seemed too much. But she managed to suppress it, replying instead with a nonchalance that matched Jack's own.

"Just a little trouble with a broom handle. Nothing Tracy couldn't manage, but thanks for asking."

Half a block later, he spoke again. "So you'll be spending the weekend in River Bend. The rooming house won't be the same without you."

"I'm flattered you think I'll be missed."

His hand on her elbow, he turned her toward him. His gaze penetrated the depths of her own. "I *know* you'll be missed," he insisted quietly. "*I'll* miss you."

Isabelle's pulse sprinted ahead three beats. She didn't know how to reply. She scrambled for words to fill the silence, but he saved her the trouble.

"I suppose we'd better get back now. I surely wouldn't

want to make Tracy angry." He tucked her hand in the crook of his elbow and walked on.

She wondered briefly if his mention of Tracy's temper had been an oblique reference to the incident in the work shed. She couldn't worry about it now, though. She had River Bend to think about.

A few silent minutes later they stood inside the back door. Isabelle released the leash from her mutt's collar, hung it on its peg, and had turned to go upstairs when Jack stepped in front of her.

"My thoughts will go with you to River Bend—and my prayers—for a safe and pleasant excursion. Good night, Isabelle."

He was gone before she could make a reply.

Sinking into her horsehair bed a quarter hour later, curious thoughts of Jack alternated with troubling memories of Tracy's outrage in the work shed. She prayed for God's peace to dwell within her and her brother, and fell asleep to dream of a River Bend home that resembled Jamisons', and a baseball diamond on a campus that could have been Erskine's twin.

The next morning at training table, conversation began with Perkins and the bad news that his ankle problem was worse than expected, and would keep him on the bench for the remainder of the season. Isabelle was glad Jack now had a permanent assignment as second baseman, but she could see from his look of concern that he was genuinely sorry about his teammate's injury.

In the pause following Perkins's bad news, Tracy deftly changed subjects to the Detroit Tigers and their previous day's win in Montgomery where McAllister had subbed for the star fielder, Elberfeld, who had quit the team for a few days to pack his furniture for removal from Nashville to Detroit. Then Stiles turned conversation to the Erskine nine, and the advantage they would gain by Tracy's trip to scout Robinson. Throughout, Isabelle thought Jack seemed quieter than usual, but her concern subsided when he repeated his wish to both her and Tracy for a safe trip.

The hours until eleven, filled with washing breakfast dishes, helping her mother put the kitchen in order, and tidying the upstairs, passed quickly. Tracy was home, bragging of success on his exam and eager for Judith's arrival, almost before Isabelle knew it. And on the dot of eleven, the Jamisons' Cadillac pulled in front of the house, followed by the Fletcher Freight Transfer wagon.

With a glance at the two modest bags at his feet, Tracy said, "Judith must be planning to stay on a while in River Bend. We surely don't need a freight wagon for our grips."

But when they reached the curb, Isabelle recognized the Jamison Hardware trademark on several kegs aboard the wagon, and realized Mr. Jamison had evidently arranged to ship goods from his Centerport factory to River Bend along with the luggage belonging to her, Tracy, and his daughter.

Tracy gave Isabelle a hand up into the tonneau, commenting on the comfortable leather seats and smooth ride compared with the hard driver's seat and stiff suspension he was accustomed to in the buckboard.

When the Cadillac approached the depot, Tracy told Judith, "I hope your father remembered to give you the train tickets before he sailed for Detroit."

Judith winked at Isabelle. "As a matter of fact, he didn't."

Tracy's color rose. "Then you'd better have your driver turn around and take us home right now!"

"Didn't Isabelle tell you?" Judith asked innocently. "Papa saved room for us in the boxcar alongside his crates." "Stop funnin' me, Judith. Do you have the tickets, or don't you?"

Recalling the arrangements Judith had described over lunch, Isabelle told Tracy, "Relax. I'm sure Mr. Jamison has made nice plans for our train passage."

Tracy scowled. "I don't exactly call a ride in a boxcar nice plans."

Evidently unable to resist further teasing, Judith said, "It won't be as bad as you think, Tracy. I'll even lend you my feather cushion."

"Just what I need," he grumbled.

Tracy remained uneasy until the driver came to a halt at a siding where a private car marked "Jamison Hardware" was located. Judith immediately led her guests aboard.

Isabelle was quite taken with the royal blue silk-covered interior, matching leather seats, and mahogany dining suite. The decor was evidently impressive enough to reduce Tracy to two words, which he repeated again and again as he ran his hand over the deep tufting of a chair.

"I'll be . . . I'll be . . . I'll be . . . "

Sinking into the chair, he pinched the back of his own hand. "Ouch! I thought I was dreaming, but this place is real!"

Isabelle chose the seat beside his—one with a view out the window—as lost for words as was her brother.

A satisfied smile on her face, Judith sat opposite them. "See, Tracy? Your sister was right. Papa *did* make nice plans." A moment later, she added, "I hope you two like medallions of beef with truffles, because that's what Rudd will be serving for luncheon, along with Princess of Wales potatoes and Sun King souffle."

Tracy shrugged. "I'm sure it will be delicious—whatever it is."

An hour later, well into his beef tenderloin, Tracy commented to Isabelle, "I wonder if we could get Mother to serve this at home."

"Sure, if you want her to spend the whole week's budget on one meal." Swallowing the final piece of her third and last melt-in-the-mouth medallion, she said, "Enjoy this now, Tracy, because come Monday, it's back to corned beef."

Judith spoke up. "Personally, I think it's marvelous what your mother does with corned beef—slicing it paper-thin and stacking it thick between slices of her home-baked pumpernickel. And that tangy mustard of hers—what does she put in it? I've never tasted anything quite like it."

Isabelle explained. "It's mother's secret recipe, handed down from her great grandmother."

"Well, anytime she'd like to earn a couple of dollars, I'll gladly pay for a copy of it."

Tracy said, "You think her corned beef and mustard are good because you don't eat them all the time. We get them at least every other week."

Pushing aside an untouched medallion, Judith said, "Even filet can become commonplace if you eat it often enough."

Isabelle pondered the wisdom of her friend's comment while Tracy inquired about the possibility of finishing off the unwanted tenderloin. The meal over, they withdrew again to the tufted leather chairs. Though Isabelle tried to complete the punched paper bookmark she was making as a gift for Mrs. Shandler, she was too taken by the view of the river, swollen from rain and rushing along its course, to keep her hands busy.

Judith opened the book she had brought along, *Brewster's Millions*, but George Barr McCutcheon's story couldn't keep her mind off Anthony and his debate, the second of two intellectual contests scheduled for the afternoon. She wished that Anthony could have traveled with her and the Dorlons and was sitting beside her now, but she understood why he chose instead to travel last night with his fellow debaters. He had explained the esprit de corps among the group, and how their strategy and confidence always improved during the hours spent together just prior to a contest.

The two fellows he had traveled with comprised a two-man team who, in the first contest of the afternoon, would face two Robinson debaters on the question of whether or not large and powerful corporations were good for the nation. The topic had been inspired by the incorporation of the International Harvester Company last August with a capital of $120,000,000. They were now producing eighty-five percent of all farm machinery in the country. The two Robinson debaters would argue that, based on past experience, industrial giants cared little for anything except profit and that only government regulation could restrain their actions. Anthony's friends would take the argument that International Harvester was proving otherwise, and bigness, like it or not, was here to stay.

Anthony's friends looked to him as their leader, and since the victory in today's contest would be determined by the total of the two-man and one-man debate scores added together, every possible opportunity was needed to improve Erskine's chances of success. Judith admired Anthony for his loyalty to his teammates. His dedication to intellectual achievements made her all the more fond of him.

She gazed out the window beside Isabelle. The wooded river vista was giving way to suburban homes. Then warehouses, storage yards, and manufactories offered groves of stacks and a haze of gray that overspread the familiar cityscape. As the train slowed down, the two-tone brick River Bend Station came into view, its gables, towers, and dormers dwarfed by the tall center clock tower which read half past two. With the debate scheduled to begin at three in the Robinson auditorium, she knew she must find the Shandlers' driver quickly upon debarking.

She had been told Townsend, Dr. Shandler's driver, would be fetching her and the Dorlons in a 1903 Cadillac, and the automobile was easy enough to locate parked beside the curb in front of the depot. But the Englishman was nowhere to be seen. Obvious, however, was the problem with the right front tire. Depleted of air, it reclined beneath its rim, a puddle of worthless black rubber. How ironic, she thought, that the very model of automotive genius that had served as the basis for Anthony's research might now become the cause of her missing his speech altogether!

CHAPTER

10

Judith twisted her gloves in nervous anticipation of Anthony's speech, thankful to have arrived in the burgundy-draped and upholstered auditorium before he had taken the podium. Providence providing, Townsend and Tracy together had mustered the strength and expertise to mount a new tire on the right front wheel, and she silently gave thanks that the Cadillac had been restored to service with relative ease.

Victory over Robinson in the debates, however, would not be achieved so readily. The first debate had concluded a few minutes prior to their arrival and moments ago, Mr. Edrick, the judge, had announced results which favored Robinson by one point. The entire burden for an overall Erskine victory now rested on Anthony's shoulders. If the judge showed no bias, she was certain he could win by more than one point difference—enough to give Erskine the edge.

But she knew from firsthand experience that many people had made up their minds about the horseless carriage. It was but a rich man's folly that would never stand the test of time or surpass its reputation as a toy, let alone become significant as a mode of transportation for the future.

Anthony rose to take the podium for the constructive

speech in the affirmative. Afterward, the Robinson debater would give the negative constructive speech, and following a few minutes' pause for note organizing, would counter Anthony's speech with the negative rebuttal. Anthony would then be granted the last say with his own rebuttal.

Now, as he stood poised to offer the opening words in the contest, she couldn't help thinking how handsome he appeared in the new gray suit her father had insisted on buying him! He looked up, pausing to locate her in the audience, and smile.

She smiled in return, flashing him their private signal for success—hands raised with index fingers interlocked.

He signaled likewise before extracting his eyeglasses from his breast pocket, settling them on his nose, and arranging his papers.

Her heart fluttered. Their friendship, though less than a month old, had deepened quickly, proving an indescribable blessing to her. At first she had worried that it was premised solely on her father's ownership of the Cadillac, but—skilled debater that Anthony was—he had convinced her in an eloquent speech that the automobile had only served as the vehicle by which their rapport would reach the profound meaning for which it was destined.

At last she could put behind her the dreadful experiences out East where her inability to attract the attention of acceptable suitors had brought on a deep sense of failure and shame. Anthony's attentions and his skill in winning the immediate approval of her folks had turned her life from hopelessness to hopefulness, from misery to joy.

He cleared his throat to speak and her thoughts focused on the words he began to deliver.

"Resolved: that the horseless carriage will replace the

horse and carriage. For the purposes of this debate, the definition of a horseless carriage shall be any self-motor machine powered by gasoline, steam, or electricity."

He consulted his notes, though Judith knew it was only from nerves. She had heard him set forth his strategy from memory several times, and listened now as he delivered it for his opponents and the judge.

"In proving that the horseless carriage will replace the horse and carriage, I will outline the development of transportation in the past century, showing through logical progression how it points to the inevitable replacement of the horse and carriage by the horseless carriage.

"I begin my historical journey in England less than a century ago—1804, to be exact—when the railway steam locomotive was invented by the Cornishman, Richard Trevithick. Only twenty-one years later, in 1825, the first railroad opened, the Stockton & Darlington. The project was conceived and engineered by the man considered to be the father of the modern railway, George Stephenson. Although few people were convinced that the future of transportation lay in the railroad in 1825, Stephenson's next project, the Liverpool & Manchester, changed many minds, and the course of history."

Judith prayed Anthony's analogy with the railroads, the foundation of his premise, would be considered logical and persuasive by Mr. Edrick, and listened intently as he continued to reveal its history.

"Stephenson overcame tremendous difficulties to complete the Liverpool & Manchester. Turnpike companies bitterly opposed his project. Horseloving country gentlemen opposed his project. And the powerful Duke of Bridgewater, whose canal had a monopoly on freight haulage, opposed his project.

"Parliamentary approval being necessary, Stephenson took his proposal before a committee of barristers who ridiculed his country ways, his imperfect English, and his outrageous claims for steam locomotives. When he had finished his argument, however, they granted a charter.

"But many obstacles to Stephenson's success remained. Aside from human opposition, he faced tremendous natural barriers. His route would pass over bridges, through deep cuts, and across a supposedly bottomless bog called Chat Moss. Few were convinced he would succeed, but succeed he did, thus changing the future of transportation for the entire world."

Listening to Anthony now, Judith wondered if too much British history had damaged his case. She lent a keen ear to his description of America's railroad history.

"In this country, Mr. Stephenson's success went neither unnoted, nor unparalleled. In the same year Stephenson opened his Stockton & Darlington Railroad, Colonel John Stevens of Hoboken, New Jersey, built a small locomotive operated by a cog-wheel and rack rail on a circular track in his back yard to prove it would work. Five years later his two sons, Robert Livingston Stevens and Edwin A. Stevens, were granted a charter from New Jersey to build the Camden & Amboy Railroad."

Anthony's next points were crucial to his case, Judith knew. She prayed he would remember to give them the emphasis they deserved.

"The Camden & Amboy established a practical monopoly between New York and Philadelphia. Though some interests *vociferously opposed it* . . . it prospered." Anthony's well-placed pause and moderate hand gestures

102

seemed to adequately drive his point home before he continued. "Soon, this successful railroad made connections with Baltimore, Washington, and Pittsburgh. Railroads flourished in other parts of America as well."

Sensing that some in the audience were on the verge of drifting off, Judith was thankful that Anthony had finally reached the midwestern portion of his railroad history and could soon tie it to the progress of automobiles.

"When William Ogden built the Galena & Chicago Railroad, Chicago refused to allow him to build a depot in town. By 1851, one hundred miles of railroad radiated out of Chicago. And by 1860 Chicago had eleven different railroads and several stations.

"In the years since, we can trace the rapid development of the railroad by tracks laid. We are all familiar with the rush to Promontory, linking East to West in 1869. In 1870, the Kansas Pacific reached Denver. In 1882, the Oregon Short Line linked Wyoming and Oregon. Other railroad companies laying tracks in the 1880s include the Texas & Pacific, the Northern Pacific, the Denver and Rio Grande, the Southern Pacific, the Santa Fe, and the Great Northern. By 1890, the miles of railroad track in America numbered 163,597. All these tracks were laid in a mere sixty-five years. By means of comparison, I now turn my attention to the horseless carriage."

Judith breathed a sigh of relief, certain that what was to come would provide a tight enough link with words already spoken to deliver a winning argument.

"The horseless carriage is *mechanically a mere infant.*" He paused to let the point sink in, his next words unhurried. "Yet already it gives the promise of developing into a giant."

With slightly faster pacing, he proceeded with the history of the automobile.

"Originally a contemporary of the steam engine, and preceding the locomotive, it suffered from persecution and neglect which resulted in its disappearance from sight for a century. The sum and substance of its progress since its reincarnation is measured by but one short decade. In 1893 there were in existence but a few experimental machines—most of them in France and a few in Germany and the United States.

"It is quite within bounds to say that the horseless carriage will do what the horse and carriage has done. It will also do the work of the railroads. Routes which accommodate the horse and carriage will serve the horseless carriage. Unlike the railroad, no specialized track need be laid. The progress of the horseless carriage in overtaking the horse and carriage—and even the railroads—in popularity will therefore move at a much more rapid pace than did the progress of the railroad.

"The horse and carriage is a highly specialized conveyance, the product of centuries of ceaseless endeavor which has resulted in bringing it to approximate perfection. Human skill and ingenuity can go but little further in that particular direction. As this nation continues into the twentieth century," he paused, the hammer of his hand adding emphasis to the words, "*something better is needed!*"

A silent moment later, he resumed a moderate pace.

"As with the railroads, Europeans have surpassed us in the advancement of the self-motor machine. Already, thousands of them are in use on the streets of Paris, predicating the eventual acceptance of their use in cities, then towns, and eventually in rural districts.

"Americans are in love with new gadgets and are ready —even eager—for a new way to get around. Aside from the novel appeal of self-motor machines, American cities in particular could benefit from the replacement of horse-drawn conveyances with this thoroughly modern mechanical device."

Judith eagerly anticipated the intriguing facts Anthony was about to reveal.

"As proof of our nation's need to move forward technically concerning self-motorized transportation, I offer the plight of New York City. Each and every day, two-and-a-half million pounds of horse manure and sixty thousand gallons of urine are deposited on its streets. In addition, each year, the carcasses of approximately fifteen thousand dead horses litter those same streets. Clearly, this demonstrates not only a tremendous problem of waste and its removal, but an enormous threat to good health as well, all of which could be eliminated by replacing horse drawn vehicles with self-motor machines.

"In considering the possibility of horseless carriages replacing horse drawn vehicles, one must not overlook the versatile nature of the self-motor machine. Just as the railroad now fulfills multiple purposes, transporting both passengers and freight, self-motor machines can and will do the same. Hitherto the automobile as a pastime or a racing machine has absorbed the lion's share of attention. This is a natural consequence of its experimental state. In this way it parallels the infancy of the railroad in America begun as a toy in the back yard of Colonel Stevens.

"But I submit that, like the railroad, the horseless carriage will prove its usefulness in business. Despite current domination of the horse-drawn wagon and the boxcar, wise businessmen will soon discover the advantages of a machine which can do the work of three horses in a fraction of the time, with a minimum of the labor, and without the restriction of special tracks."

Arrested by the increasing strength of Anthony's argument, Judith sat stock still as he continued to set forth his premise.

"The self-motor machine goes at any desired speed—equaling at will the horse in slowness, the locomotive in swiftness. It is always ready, can start on a journey of one mile or a thousand at a moment's notice, needs but one person to operate it and provides accommodations for either passengers or—if so desired—freight. The choice of routes is world-wide, and it can rise superior to considerations of weather. In short, there are no bounds to its capabilities, no appreciable limit to its usefulness.

"In considering the permanency of the self-motor vehicle on the transportation scene, the horse and carriage invites comparison. Much that is said in commendation of the self-motor machine applies with equal force to the horse and carriage. However, the self-motor machine does all that the horse and carriage does and without dependence on the strength of a four-legged animal. It is a machine—a mechanical device whose energies are not bound by the limits of muscle, sinew, and bone—its proclivities not subject to the whims and fears of the equine mind.

"Neither is its radius limited to that of the horse and carriage. The owner of a pair of horses in the country may be said to have a practical everyday radius of about twelve miles. With an automobile of ten horsepower, the radius for a family or businessman is comfortably thirty miles.

Calculating the square miles within a day's drive, the automobile owner has available to him more than six times the territory of a horse and buggy driver. And today, the automobile is thoroughly efficient and reliable."

Judith prayed Anthony's somewhat controversial claim wouldn't be considered unfounded. He hastened to follow up the premise.

"The automobile is the cheapest vehicle in existence, initial cost and operating expenses being considered. The value of the annual product of automobiles in the United States alone reaches tens of millions of dollars and it is only in its first decade of development!

"Carriage manufacturers are already switching over to the production of horseless carriages. Many of them are in the experimental stage, to be sure, but as they proceed in the great tradition of American ingenuity, they will develop ever more sophisticated and serviceable machines to serve their customers, gradually relegating the horse drawn buggy to obsolescence."

Now, Judith prayed that the close of Anthony's argument would be as persuasive as his previously delivered words.

"Just as customers for railroad service have multiplied in geometric proportions, the clientele for self-motor machines will grow and grow. The day will come when the poor man will have his automobile as surely as the rich man. He will use it to bring his home and his work shop close together, and also for his outings. A house without an automobile will be the exception. The automobile will become an indispensable adjunct to modern civilization."

Judith drew a short, quick breath. The auditorium remained silent, save the shuffling of papers as Anthony prepared to leave the podium. She began to clap her hands, a lonely sound that reverberated off the walls of the near-empty auditorium. Isabelle, then Tracy added their applause to hers, but they could raise only a thin veneer of support as Anthony stepped down to take his seat.

His opponent, a short, chunky fellow introduced by the moderator as Harold Harmon, stepped onto a riser put in place behind the podium and dabbed his forehead with his handkerchief. As he drew a breath to speak, Judith hoped his argument would be less convincing, his delivery less impressive than Anthony's, but as she listened to his opening statement, she found no reason to believe that such would be the case.

CHAPTER

11

Harold Harmon's voice rang with confidence.

"I stand before you to prove that the horseless carriage cannot and will not ever replace the horse and carriage. I will do so by describing the logical future of transportation in this country, by citing the practical reasons why the horseless carriage will not dominate, and by offering real examples of legal and emotional resistance to such a possibility."

Impressed by his intelligent, insightful approach, Judith feared Anthony may have met his match. She listened keenly as Mr. Harmon continued.

"I begin with the current state of transportation in America. Railroads offer city-to-city, state-to-state, and cross-country service which is both affordable and efficient for the vast majority of passengers and freight. Such efficiency and economy precludes the dominance of any other mode of transportation for the foreseeable future.

"While it is true trains are limited by the destination of

their tracks, it is also true that even as I speak, more miles of track are being laid. Within the next few years, even the smallest bergs and remotest villages will be connected to the major rail lines currently in operation. In fact, I predict that the expansion of the rail system in the United States of America will never cease, because for every new town that springs up in a location not served by trains, new connections will be laid to the nearest major rail line."

Judith shuddered at the strength of Mr. Harmon's logic and prayed that as his argument progressed, Anthony would find weaknesses she couldn't see.

Harmon proceeded confidently. "Where rail service cannot suffice, such as within the limits of big cities, other means of travel have come to the fore. Trolley cars, inter-urbans, elevated railways, and even underground railways transport travelers safely, efficiently, and economically. I hold that these metropolitan and inter-urban means of travel have done and will do more to replace the horse and carriage than any other force, in particular the self-motor machine.

"But the demise of horse drawn vehicles is folly for other reasons. For centuries, a significant portion of the world's economy, and that of America's, has resulted from the fact that skilled men are paid for their expertise in breeding, training, dealing, and driving horseflesh. Can we possibly predict the eradication of such a vast and thriving segment of our country's worth?"

Judith had never given this point a thought. She desperately hoped Anthony had.

Having paused to consult his note cards, Harmon expanded on his point. "Many other practical reasons force the conclusion that the self-motor machine will not rise to prominence on the transportation scene. One simple reason is this: a self-motor machine cannot even rise to the top of a hill!"

Harmon's humor elicited quiet chuckles from his audience, but what tickled Judith was the erroneous nature of his claim. She listened eagerly to hear how he would back up his faulty point.

"I cite as an example the experiences of a gentleman in my hometown of Rose Arbor a mere fifty miles from here. Mr. Edward Staebler has been trying for three years to establish an automobile dealership in addition to his coal, seed, farm machinery, and cycle business. In so doing, he purchased a self-motor machine called a Trimoto. With it, he encountered *all manner of problems*.

"After one month of use, the plate attached to the bottom of the chimney in the carburetor broke loose and had to be returned to the factory in Chicago. After the repair, it immediately broke a second time.

"As I mentioned earlier, the engine itself did not have sufficient power to climb the hills in Rose Arbor. Mr. Staebler also noticed that, after only about three hundred miles of use, the brakes were beginning to wear out the tires, so he returned his Trimoto to the factory in Chicago. Even though the company made repairs and improvements, the Trimoto never could climb the hills, nor could Mr. Staebler sell the machine to any of several dealers who witnessed a demonstration of its abilities, or lack thereof. He finally turned it back in to the company for credit against a different automobile.

"Mr. Staebler next acquired a Toledo Steam Carriage. Soon after, it began to give trouble. The air-pressure pump quit and the gasoline line grew plugged. Shortly after these

111

problems arose, the left rear wheel shaft loosened up. Mr. Staebler had only just repaired the problem when two bolts which adjust the drive chain snapped off. When Mr. Staebler was ready to drive the car to Toledo for the installation of an improved chain and adjustment, the water coil in the boiler sprang a leak. He was thirteen miles from home, which necessitated the hiring of a *horse* to tow him to his destination."

Again, the audience laughed, and Judith with them, for she knew that Anthony could successfully counter the one-man's-troubles scenario.

Harmon continued on his theme. "Mr. Staebler, keeping faith with the concept of the self-motor machine and the Toledo Steam Carriage Company, shipped his automobile by rail for repairs. He drove it for only a few days after it had been returned to him from the factory, then encountered more trouble.

"The connecting rod broke off near the crank end, bent the crank, and broke the case. Also, the steam would sometimes blow through the engine without moving it. His carriage was repaired, but a few days later, a water pipe in the boiler sprang a leak.

"This was not by any means his only problem. The tires were being cut by the rims. The steering knuckles were bent. The arm behind the front axle rattled. The packing for the valve passing through the cup on the pilot light leaked.

"When the factory in Toledo had repaired the machine, Mr. Staebler went there to drive it home. He started out at 11:25 in the morning and arrived in Rose Arbor, fifty-eight miles away, at 7:30 that evening. He made no better time than if he were to be drawn by a horse, but he consumed eleven gallons of gasoline and a quart of cylinder and lubricating oil.

"Perhaps the most telling part of Mr. Staebler's experience is this. After much effort to keep his automobile operating, and many demonstrations given to interested parties, he was unable to sell any horseless carriages by the close of 1901. He blamed the lateness of the season in part. With roads turning bad, he had to wait until the following spring. The fact that automobiles cannot be run on unpaved roads during winter months lends one more point to my argument that they will never replace the horse and carriage.

"And I can cite further practical reasons why the self-motor machine will never dominate our roadways. They will rob work from coachmen, horse breeders, and horse dealers. And I must insert here that, referring to a point made by my opponent, they will also put out of work the thousands of gentlemen now employed to clean the streets of our cities."

Judith was impressed by the manner in which Harold Harmon had seemingly turned Anthony's point to his own favor, but she was certain it would be successfully rebutted. She listened closely as he continued.

"Even though a great loss of employment would result from the popularity of self-motor machines and impose a great threat to the health of our nation's economy, one needn't worry for a moment that such will be the case. The reason is this: motor-driven vehicles are simply too costly for the common citizen to own. Any self-respecting farmer with $750 to spend on transportation will find himself a good team of driving horses which will be undeterred by cold weather and sloppy roads.

"Farmers know, too, that self-motor machines cannot feasibly share roads with horses without causing all manner of inconvenience and calamity to horseback riders and carriage drivers whose animals are unaccustomed to their noise and speed. According to the Farm Journal, automobiles are noisy, smoking stink wagons designed to frighten to death anything they can't flatten out. And I quote: 'The very sight of one is enough to dry up a whole dairy herd.'"

Judith should have anticipated that a student at Robinson, known for its agricultural department, would eventually draw the plight of the farmer into his argument. She hoped Anthony had prepared a counter-attack.

Harmon went on. "The Medical Journal predicts: 'If the machine ever attains the unlikely speed of eighty miles per hour, it will have to drive itself, for the human brain will be incapable of controlling it.'"

In the pause that followed, Judith repressed a snigger, certain the quote must be outdated.

"And now I turn to the laws currently governing the use of automobiles. Politicians agree that if they cannot barricade their streets against the use of these snorting, hissing demons, they had better enlarge our hospitals for their victims, and our penitentiaries for their drivers.

"As an example of this attitude in practice, I offer the laws of Smithton, Pennsylvania, where any self-propelled vehicle must come to a complete halt upon approaching a crossroad. The engineer must thoroughly examine the roadway ahead and sound his horn vigorously, then holler hello loudly or ring a bell after which he must fire a gun of sufficient caliber to be heard a great distance. Thereupon he will dismount and discharge a Roman candle, firecracker, or some other explosive device as final warning of his approach.

"And in the State of Indiana, a motorist scaring a team of horses into bolting can be fined up to $100 for each runaway mile. If the horse balks at the car altogether, the motorist must discharge his passengers and convince the horse that the car isn't there by covering it with a cloth resembling the surrounding countryside. If the horse *still* balks, the driver must take his machine apart as quickly as possible and conceal the pieces in the grass along the side of the road.

"Many communities have secret speed limits and scorching traps where speeders are caught. The reason for this is because automobilists are notorious for driving their machines too fast.

"In Yonkers, Magistrate Kellogg has a squad of bicycling cops to control speeding automobilists. On Chicago's North Shore Drive, policemen shoot at motorists who disobey speed laws. Many other municipalities will be forced to institute similar laws to control fanatic motor car drivers.

"In conclusion, I claim again that the horseless carriage cannot and will not ever replace the horse and carriage. The future of transportation in this country will be along the lines of the railroad, trolleys, and interurbans which are ever expanding the miles of tracks they lay, and therefore the number of customers they serve.

"The horseless carriage is an impractical machine suitable only for the privileged minority interested in pleasure driving, and then only on flat roadways during warm months of the year where no horses or cows can be found.

"Finally, resistance to the motor machine is so powerful that ever more laws will be written to ban them from use,

115

relegating them to the junk heap of bad ideas."

As Harold Harmon left the podium, his supporters erupted in loud shouts of praise and thundering applause that reverberated throughout the auditorium.

Judith chewed her lip. The Robinson debater had presented an argument which seemed to match Anthony's in strength, and he had the advantage of defending the status quo, always more appealing to the human spirit than the prospect of change.

The applause died away and the moderator stood to announce a ten-minute recess while Mr. Harmon prepared his rebuttal speech. Judith glanced at Anthony, bent grim-faced over the desk arm of his chair. He was writing furiously, making notes for his own rebuttal. She prayed his words in defense of his position would give Erskine the edge. Well she knew that a win today would mean more than just a victory. It would wipe away a year's worth of disappointment over the narrow defeat at their previous encounter at Erskine.

Too anxious to sit still, Judith invited Isabelle and Tracy to join her in catching a breath of fresh air outside. The Dorlons followed her up the aisle and out the main entrance where the low angle of the afternoon sun cast elongated shadows of cedars against the wide brick walkway. Taking a deep breath, she tried to appreciate the chirps of the sparrows and songs of the robins, but their melodies couldn't drown out worrisome thoughts over the outcome of today's match. Minutes later, she returned to her seat between Isabelle and Tracy, each of whom offered an encouraging smile before focusing attention once again on Mr. Harmon.

He sipped from a glass of water, then commenced his

rebuttal.

"Ladies and gentlemen, distinguished judge, you've heard my opponent give a long and detailed account of the history of the railroad from its infancy to its current state, then switch it to a one-way track destined for obsolescence. What he failed to tell you, however, is that the history of the automobile, the very instrument he claims will bring down the power of the rails, actually precedes the invention of the train.

"I speak of the *Orukter Amphibolos*, or the Amphibious Digger invented in 1805 by Mr. Oliver Evans for the city of Philadelphia. Its purpose was to dredge the Schuylkill River and clean the city docks. Its appearance, unlike self-motored carriages of today, was that of a scow twelve feet wide and thirty feet long. In it was mounted a steam engine producing five horse power. The combined weight of both the engine and its odd carriage totaled fifteen-and-a-half tons, thus causing the first set of wheels to break down.

"Much to the credit of Mr. Evans and his crew, a second set of wheels of sufficient strength to bear this ponderous weight, was constructed and fitted onto the machine. During the second week of July, this clumsy contraption moved under its own power down Center Street much to the amusement and—I'm sure—the amazement of his fellow Philadelphians.

"The fact that Mr. Evans managed to invent a steam road vehicle which actually worked should come as no great surprise. His fascination with the concept predated the American Revolution. On the day that his steam-driven scow made its public appearance, he even offered to wager $3000 that he could build a steam-powered vehicle that would travel faster than any horse in the world.

"But his wager had no takers, and for good reason. His idea was a bad one. Even Philadelphians of 1805 recognized that. In fact, the idea was so ill-conceived that until his death in 1819, Mr. Evans never again secured financing to produce a self-motor machine. "His dream seemed to have died with him, and should have stayed dead. Had it been worth pursuing, surely some Yankee entrepreneur would have backed him with enough money to create another self-powered machine. Instead, neither the public nor financiers were much impressed. And until ten years ago, the concept of self-motor machines remained dormant in this country.

"Despite revived interest on the part of some, several businessmen have already investigated and dismissed the concept of building horseless carriages. Some of the automobile manufacturers who have gone into business and already quit making self-motor machines are Akron, Baldwin, Chicago, Detroit Steamer, Eddy Electric, Gasmobile, Halsey, Imperial, Jackson, Krastin, Lane Steamer, Milwaukee Steam, Prospect, Quick, Rogers, Samuels Electric, Turner, United Motor, Victor Steam, Western—and there are many more. The newspapers are full of reports naming them.

"Returning again to the point of reliability, I have already listed in detail Mr. Staebler's troubles. Had time permitted, I could have told you of others whose experiences paralleled his. The scenario has been repeated across the country dozens upon dozens of times by hopeful, but ill-advised men whose efforts to find alternatives to the horse and buggy are sadly misdirected.

"So in conclusion, I state again that the horseless carriage will never replace the horse and carriage owing to poorly-conceived designs which can never be perfected. History has proven my point over a ninety-eight year span of time. The continuing expansion of railroads, interurbans, and trolleys which have a solid track record for safety, efficiency, and economy, will continue to serve the majority of our country's transportation needs."

As Harold Harmon collected his notes, praise issued forth from his supporters.

"Bravo, Harmon!"

"You've done it!"

"Victory to Robinson!"

The snide smile on Harmon's face as he stepped down from his platform disgusted Judith. She chewed her lip as Anthony took his place, heartened somewhat by the fact that he appeared completely confident.

He carefully arranged his notes, then focused on the judge. "I would like to begin my remarks by taking up a point my opponent made regarding coachmen, horse breeders, dealers, and others dependent upon the performance and exchange of horseflesh. Permit me to quote Sir Isaac Coffin in his deliberations in Parliament.

"'What will become of coach-makers and harness-makers, coach-masters and coachmen, inn-keepers, horse-breeders and horse dealers? Is the house aware of the smoke and noise, the hiss and whirl which engines passing at the rate of ten or twelve miles an hour will occasion? Neither the cattle plowing in the field or grazing in the meadows can behold them without dismay. It will be the greatest nuisance, the most complete disturbance of quiet and comfort in all parts of the kingdom that the ingenuity of man can invent.'"

Anthony paused, put aside the page from which he'd

been reading, then focused on his opponent. "Mr. Coffin made his speech—not in 1896 when Parliament was deliberating on the regulation of motor cars—but in *1826* when the monster that was purportedly ready to throw men out of work was the railway engine. Throughout history, man has proven that with every new invention, even though some workers are temporarily replaced by machines, they eventually become employed manufacturing or tending to the very machines which replaced them. Should the rise in popularity of the motor car be any different?

"For example: men who now drive horses for their employers will instead drive horseless carriages. Men who now make harnesses, saddles, wagon wheels, and the like will go on to manufacture steering gears, automobile wheels, seats, and more."

Directing his next comment to the judge, Anthony said, "As for my opponent's point that laws discriminate against self-motor machines, he is perfectly correct. Ordinances requiring drivers to fire off guns and the like, constitute highway robbery because if you obeyed them, the authorities could put the arm on you for disturbing the peace, sabbath-breaking, illegal transportation of explosives, and discharging firearms within town limits. *Such laws will not stand.*

"As proof, I offer the sage words of Judge Russell from the State of New York, who two years ago had the foresight and wisdom to express this learned opinion. And I quote:

"'The day is past in the history of New York State when we are obliged to give up the use of highways entirely to the use of carriages propelled by horses or oxen. Whatever we may think about the value of steam carriages or carriages propelled by electricity or any other motive power aside from animal power, the time has come when those carriages have a right to go on the public highways for reasons perhaps of utility as well as pleasure . . .' End quote.

"Granted, those who oppose self-motor machines on public roadways currently outnumber those who favor the rights of automobilists, but the tables will turn. The popularity of the self-motor machine is growing too rapidly to be stopped. As proof, I offer the interest evident at the New York Automobile show this past January.

"There, Mr. William E. Metzger tended the display of the Cadillac, and by mid-week declared the model sold out, for he had already taken orders for 2286 vehicles of Mr. Leland's design. This testifies to the success of *only one of the dozens of automobiles* on display at the show.

"As for automobile manufacturers quitting business, for every one my opponent named, I can name three who are staying in business or starting one up. I, too, have compiled a list of names which I haven't time to read." He held up a paper as proof of his claim.

"And now I would like to speak to the point my opponent made about the unreliability of the automobile, and their inability to climb hills. I offer as counterpoint the examples of three individuals: Mr. Jamison of Centerport, and Dr. Shandler and Judge Whittaker of River Bend.

"Three weeks ago Mr. Jamison took delivery of a new Cadillac. Since that time, his automobile has never failed to perform. It climbs hills easily. It runs on rough roads. It starts, stops, turns, and backs up with equal ease. And the machine has neither broken any parts nor failed to perform.

"I know what you're thinking. Three weeks hardly constitutes a satisfactory test period. I therefore offer you the examples of Judge Whittaker and Dr. Shandler of this

121

fair city.

"Judge Whittaker purchased an '01 Oldsmobile two years ago, drove it extensively about the area, and found it to be such a sound machine, he recently purchased an '03 Oldsmobile as well.

"Dr. Shandler took delivery of his Cadillac three months ago. Since that time, he has experienced no break-downs."

Judith caught her breath at Anthony's claim—now false, unbeknownst to him.

His laudatory comments continued. "Instead, Dr. Shandler has enjoyed all of the conveniences of a machine able to perform when called upon. His Cadillac carries him and his family to church each week; his driver uses it to run errands for Mrs. Shandler daily; and he uses it to transport Mrs. Shandler and some of her friends to the meetings of various civic and women's organizations. The machine is so satisfactory that Mrs. Shandler's women friends have all urged their own husbands to place their names on a waiting list for the new model Cadillac planned for next year.

Focusing directly on Harold Harmon, Anthony said, "Dr. Shandler and Judge Whittaker and their automobiles have been much in evidence on the streets of River Bend, and their successes with motor machines have been the subject of frequent comment in the *River Bend Tribune*."

Shifting his gaze to the judge, he added, "I'm surprised my worthy opponent failed to grant this point in his own speech."

Pausing to consult his notes, Anthony continued his remarks to the judge. "In summation, I claim to have proven that the horseless carriage is indeed destined to replace its horse-drawn counterpart. Men displaced from livelihoods derived from the breeding, training, driving, and selling of horseflesh will take up new employment in the fledgling automobile industry. Lawmakers resistant to the rights of automobilists will fold beneath the pressure of ever-growing numbers of horseless carriage drivers insistent on equal access to roadways. Poorly designed and performing models of self-motor machines will disappear beneath the rising tide of well-engineered and reliable machines. And good old-fashioned American ingenuity—along with the manufacturing experience of Mr. Henry Martyn Leland and the engineering prowess of Ransom Eli Olds—will eventually provide the public with self-motor machines affordable to the average man who will make them the transportation of choice on our nation's roadways."

As Anthony folded his notes and tucked them in his pocket, Judith led her three-person support team in a round of applause that, thin though it was, earned a nod of appreciation from the recipient. By the time Anthony had stepped down from the podium, Judith could see that the judge was furiously marking his ballot form.

Anthony headed directly to where his opponent was seated. Harold rose to shake hands and the two spent a minute in conversation before the other debaters from both sides surrounded their respective teammates to offer moral support. A few minutes later, Anthony parted from his friends to join Judith.

She greeted him with a tentative smile—a reflection of Anthony's own expression—and the one question she couldn't help asking. "Do you think you've convinced the judge that the horseless carriage is here to stay?"

He lifted his shoulders. "Harmon put up a strong

argument for his case. But he knows Mr. Edrick from other debates and says he's unquestionably fair. We'll simply have to wait."

Tracy clapped Anthony on the shoulder. "No matter what the results, you put forth a commendable effort. No one can fault you there."

Isabelle concurred. "You've represented Erskine admirably."

Anthony nodded appreciatively. Taking Judith by the hand, he said to her and the Dorlons, "Come meet my teammates. It could take Mr. Edrick some time to complete his forms. We might as well all wait together."

The other Erskine debaters stood at the foot of the stage, already engaged in an earnest discussion with the Robinson team over the future of the automobile.

Anthony tried to make introductions, but the attention of his debating friends, Lon and Raymond, was so focused on the controversial subject, they barely acknowledged Judith's presence. Points and counterpoints filled the air while she listened in amazement.

A Robinson debater said, "Man will never learn to love a machine. A horse, you can love. But what is a machine?"

Lon countered. "Man *already* loves machines."

Raymond added, "He's been in love with them since the start of the industrial revolution over a century ago."

Another Robinson fellow responded. "I'll grant you man loves machines—machines that do work and make life easier."

Harmon spoke up. "That's right. You sure can't claim that for automobiles. For the most part, they just make life miserable!"

Anthony grinned. "Can I quote you on that twenty years from now when you're driving down Main Street in a brand new motor machine that takes you all the way across town in less time than it takes to hitch up a team?"

His opponent smiled and wagged his finger. "You can quote me on it!"

Other arguments were mounted and rebutted until Mr. Edrick approached, ballots in hand. Students parted to make a place for him in their midst.

Focusing in turn on Harold and Anthony, he said, "Each of you mounted strong arguments for your side, earning you the highest compliment I can offer. You've made my job very difficult. But the score can't end in a tie, so . . . "

CHAPTER

12

All eyes focused on Edrick. Not a soul stirred. Judith held her breath, a silent prayer going out on Erskine's behalf.

Edrick's gaze shifted from Anthony to Harold and back again.

Offering his hand to Anthony, he said, "Congratulations, son. You're the winner, forty-eight points to Mr. Harmon's forty-six."

Recognizing overall victory in the two-point spread, the Erskine team erupted in cheers. Anthony hugged Judith so hard, the stays of her corset jammed painfully against her ribs, but she didn't mind. The man she admired had earned a hard-fought victory for his school and she couldn't remember ever being happier than she was at this moment.

Isabelle, watching Anthony and Judith embrace in a victory celebration, couldn't help smiling over the friendship that had grown so quickly since the day she had served them tea in her mother's parlor. Her thought was interrupted when Tracy nudged her, a grin on his face as he nodded in the direction of the aisle behind them.

There, less than a dozen feet away, stood a fellow she had never expected to see in River Bend.

"Jack! How did you get here?"

He closed the gap between them. "On the train, same as you!"

"But—"

"I decided it was time to visit my aunt and uncle, the ones I stayed with when I attended high school and business college. I was going to wait until tomorrow and just come for the game, then I changed my mind."

Tracy gave Jack a friendly nudge. "Couldn't stay away, eh, Weatherby?" His gaze shifted to Isabelle and back again.

Warmth suffused her cheeks. "I doubt very much that Jack's presence here has anything to do with—"

Her protest was interrupted by Judith. "Here comes Dr. Shandler!" She indicated a white-haired gentleman descending the aisle at a snappy pace.

He greeted Judith with a fatherly hug, a kiss on the cheek, and an accent that sounded like he'd just departed the foggy shores of England. "Jolly good to see you again, my dear!" Blue eyes sparkling, he added, "I came straight away from the hospital hoping to take in some of the debate, but I seem to be—"

Judith interrupted excitedly. "Erskine won, thanks to Anthony!"

Dr. Shandler extended his hand. "Congratulations, my boy! Jolly good! Jolly good, indeed!"

Anthony beamed. "I credit you in part for the victory. Your trouble-free experience with your Cadillac lent great strength to my argument."

Judith's brow arched. "Anthony, I have something to tell you later." To Dr. Shandler, she said, "Let us introduce you to everyone."

When Isabelle, Tracy, Jack, and Anthony's fellow

debaters, Lon and Raymond, had been properly introduced, Dr. Shandler said, "This calls for a victory celebration. Anthony, Lon, Raymond, Jack—come along home with us for dinner."

The debaters exchanged nods.

Anthony said, "Thank you, sir. That sounds appreciably better than the cheap meal the three of us were planning at the closest diner."

Jack said, "I have to ring my aunt and uncle and let them know I won't be taking dinner with them."

Dr. Shandler told him, "You can ring them up the instant we arrive home." Starting up the aisle, he said, "Follow me. We live just up the street, no more than ten minutes from here."

Judith laughed. "Don't believe him! It's a mile away, and it's tucked so far back off the street you'd never find it unless you'd been there before."

As the entourage emerged from the auditorium, Isabelle was thankful to have Jack by her side. Paying little heed to the swift pace of the others, they fell behind as she told him of Mr. Jamison's private car, the trouble with the Shandler Cadillac, and the course of the debate. Suddenly realizing that the others were no longer in sight, Isabelle panicked.

"Where did they go? Did you see? Now we're lost and it's all my fault!" Her heart raced.

"We're not lost," Jack assured her, pointing to the crest of a wooded hill. "They turned right up there."

Hardly listening, she hurried up the hill, horrified that her worst nightmare had come true and that she was lost in a strange city. Jack kept pace with her, but she scarcely noticed, too haunted by Judith's words, . . . *you'd never find it unless you'd been there before,* which ran through

128

her mind again and again.

She had arrived at the top of the hill and was ready to start down the other side when Jack nabbed her by the elbow.

"Not so fast! They turned here." He indicated a twisting drive through the pine woods so camouflaged by thick junipers that Isabelle had walked right past without even noticing it.

She followed Jack. Eventually, the evergreens opened up to an artfully composed set of roofs thrusting from the second story of a Queen Ann home. The place was just as Judith had described it when she had come to help Isabelle pack. It had pale blue siding of horizontal clapboards, fish scale shingles, and ornamental floral carving. The porch was supported by beautifully turned spindle work accented with gingerbread and adorned by English ivy.

Together, she and Jack climbed the steps.

They were met at the door by a maid capped in white. "The others are in the parlor. Follow me," she said with a pleasant smile.

Remembering his aunt and uncle, Jack said, "Excuse me, ma'am, but could you please show me to the telephone? I need to ring up my aunt and uncle."

"Right this way."

The maid led them to the telephone in the front parlor, leaving them with directions to the back parlor where the others had congregated. While Jack was making his call, Isabelle stepped into the hall, trying to follow the instructions—and the sound of cheerful voices—to the back parlor. But she soon became confused and decided to wait for Jack instead.

The friendly faces of their chums offered a bright

accompaniment to the lavender and Wedgwood blue sitting room with its Reticella lace curtains, leaded glass windows, and forget-me-not floral carpet. Dr. Shandler added two Eastlake straightbacked chairs to the occupied sofa, love seat, and easy chairs.

A honey-haired woman at least twenty years younger than the doctor rose to greet them.

"Welcome! I'm Mrs. Shandler. You must be Miss Dorlon and Mr. Weatherby."

Before they could answer, a thirteen-year-old boy sprang to his feet, his blue eyes shining. "And I'm Sheridan Shandler."

Isabelle offered her hand to mother and son in turn.

Before the boy had finished shaking her hand, he said, "Do you know what a guest and a fish have in common?"

His mother scowled. "Sheridan! What a dreadful thing to ask!"

Remembering Judith's coaching from yesterday, Isabelle told the boy, "After three days, they start to go stale." With a grin, she added, "But you needn't worry, Sheridan. I have no intention of staying past Sunday."

When she and Jack had been seated, Dr. Shandler said, "We were just discussing our favorite humorists. Mine is Mark Twain."

Sheridan said, "And mine is Benjamin Franklin."

Isabelle said, "He was the author of your riddle about guests and fish, was he not?"

Sheridan shook his head. "He borrowed it from earlier versions by Plautus and Lyly, but you're clever to know Mr. Franklin had said it, too." After a moment's contemplation, he added, "In fact, Miss Dorlon, you're not only clever, you're pretty! And I doubt very much you'd go stale after three days!"

Everyone laughed, most of all Dr. Shandler. He was still chuckling when a stunning young lady of about eighteen strolled into the parlor, her shiny amber hair piled casually into a thick knot atop her head. "Sorry I'm late. I seem to be missing all the fun."

Dr. Shandler rose to greet her with a kiss on each cheek. "Serena, meet our guests."

As he worked his way around the room, reciting the names with perfect accuracy, Isabelle noticed that Tracy's focus never strayed from the charming beauty. Her slender figure was further enhanced by the latest fashion in skirts— box plaits stitched to flounce length in slot-seam style.

Introductions over, he nearly sprang from his chair. "Take my seat, Miss Shandler. I'll fetch another."

He was back within seconds, parking his chair beside Serena's and listening intently as she shared news of the day's experiences at the local hospital where she was volunteering as an aid to the nurses.

Afterward, Dr. Shandler asked each guest to tell a little about him or herself. When all had spoken, Mrs. Shandler announced that dinner would be served in fifteen minutes, then showed Isabelle and Judith to the bedroom and bath they would share in the guest suite, and Tracy to his own room and bath across the hall.

The girls' bedroom was just where Judith had described it, down the hall to the left of the main entrance. But it was far more accommodating than Isabelle had anticipated. The deep rose color of the walls and matching carpet immediately instilled in her a sense of wellbeing, chasing away the last of her apprehensions over the trip to River Bend. Matching beds with white eyelet spreads dominated two parallel walls. A vanity had been set in between. Against the left wall was a blue Empire Transitional love seat occupied by a family of bisque dolls, the prettiest of which appeared to be a likeness of Serena, even down to the costume she was wearing today.

Isabelle's bag had already been delivered and unpacked, as had Judith's. When they had refreshed themselves, Isabelle led the way back to the sitting room, pleased to have found it without any confusion, wrong turns, or help from Judith. Within minutes, a gong summoned all to the dining room where cream-colored wall paper, Jacobean-patterned carpet, and an ecru cut work tablecloth edged with filet lace softened the formality of the gold-banded china and sterling silver laid at each place. The most arresting feature of the room, however, was its wide window offering a panoramic view of the river.

Here, the pines gave way to a terraced bank planted in roses and perennials that would eventually bloom forth. Tile steps offered easy descent to a dock where two canoes were tied up. Isabelle couldn't have asked for a prettier scene as she took her place across from Sheridan at the dinner table.

The cuisine soon proved to be as unique as the view. The main dish of salmon balls in remoulade sauce offered a tasty change from the meals Isabelle was accustomed to serving at her mother's table. Dessert was a special treat, too, a Princess Eugenie pudding featuring lemon flavoring, coconut, and a delicate raspberry sauce.

The meal over, Dr. Shandler escorted his guests down the pathway to the river. High above the water, a pair of swallows swooped and darted off, catching insects for their evening meal.

132

Leading the way onto the dock, Sheridan said, "Father, may we please take out the canoes?"

He nodded. "I was just going to suggest that very thing."

Sheridan's face lit with excitement. "Let's have a race! Mr. Dorlon, Mr. Weatherby—what do you say we take on Mr. Tidball and his debaters?"

Seeing the momentary dread in Jack's eyes, Isabelle said, "Mr. Weatherby is taking me on a walk along the river. Dr. Shandler, why don't you go instead?"

"As you wish."

Serena said, "Judith and I will officiate. The first team to circle the big rock in the bend and paddle back to the dock, wins!"

Seconds later, when the boats were filled with competitors and untied, Judith said in loud, clear tones, "Ready, set, go!"

They pushed off, water splashing when six paddles hit the river. As the canoeists made their way upstream, Jack led Isabelle in the opposite direction, along a manicured path that bordered the Shandlers' extensive riverfront property.

Relieved to have escaped a delicate situation, he paused near a granite boulder that formed the centerpiece of a rock garden and turned to her. Taking her hands in his, he searched her brown eyes. "Thank you for suggesting the walk, Isabelle. You saved me an inning of embarrassment."

All too familiar with humiliation suffered from shortcomings, she replied, "It seemed the best thing to say at the moment." Squeezing his hands, she added, "One day soon, when you've learned to swim, you needn't ever be embarrassed again."

He offered a narrow smile. "One day soon." Keeping her hand in his, he strolled a little farther, then paused to face her again. "By the way, you were wrong."

"But you just said—"

"Not about the canoeing. This afternoon, when you started to tell Tracy you didn't think my presence in River Bend had anything to do with you. You were wrong."

Isabelle's pulse quickened as she searched his deep blue eyes, waiting for further explanation.

It came softly, like the caress of his finger now gently tracing her cheekbone. "My presence here has *everything* to do with you."

Her voice barely breaking a whisper, she said, "Knowing how devoted you are to baseball, I assumed . . . " Her words trailed off as the distant shouts of Sheridan Shandler proclaimed his team the winners of the race. But Jack didn't seem to hear them.

He stood so near, she could feel the warmth of his breath as he spoke. "There was a time not long ago when you would have been right. But things are different now. Being with you—"

Again, the sound of Sheridan Shandler's voice, emanating from his canoe, echoed off the water.

"Mr. Weatherby! Miss Dorlon! Are you sure you don't want a ride in my canoe?"

Irritated by the interruption, Jack nevertheless remained polite. "Not tonight, Sheridan. Thanks anyway."

When he focused again on Isabelle, the tender moment had vanished, along with the sentiments he had planned to share.

Sensing his frustration, Isabelle said, "I suppose it's

time we headed back."

Dusk was beginning to move in as they joined the others at the dock and followed Dr. Shandler to the house. "Let's go into the library, shall we? I have some volumes there that I think you young people will find quite interesting."

Apprehension built within at every step carrying Isabelle closer to the roomful of books. Judith, pausing outside the door, took her aside to speak in privacy.

"I'd forgotten how much Dr. Shandler enjoys showing off his collection of rare editions. He loves to hear readings from them, too. Maybe we should go to our room now. It's been a long day."

Praying for sufficient grace to reckon with her inadequacies, and the strength to accept them in the way her mother had advised, she told Judith, "I'd just as soon join the others, if you don't mind."

"As you wish."

Recognizing uneasiness in Judith, Isabelle strode with false confidence into the room, claiming the empty chair between Tracy and Jack.

The fawn walls, dark oak book cases, and oxblood-colored leather chairs provided dour contrast to the enthusiastic words of Dr. Shandler as he selected volumes of literature from his vast collection.

"The English language is a thing of beauty, and I love nothing better than to hear readings from England's finest authors!"

Seeing a small black volume in his father's hand, Sheridan jumped up from his chair. "Father, may I read from that one, please? You know it's my very favorite."

Dr. Shandler complied, explaining, "This is *The Exeter*

Book. It contains ninety-five riddles. We'll see who can solve them!"

When Dr. Shandler had chosen other literary treasures for each of his guests and *Canterbury Tales* for himself, Isabelle found herself staring down at a small book containing Sir Thomas Malory's works. Though she had listened to Tracy's readings from the Arthurian Cycle earlier in the semester and could make out the title of the first part, *Slander and Strife,* the other words on the page were all a-jumble. Glancing to her left, she saw that Tracy was holding a copy of *Beowulf.* On her right, Jack was leafing through a collection of Shakespeare's sonnets. She wondered what she would do when her turn came to read, then, an idea came to her—an idea inspired by past assignments her brother had shared with her from his British Literature class.

Tracy shifted uneasily in his chair. Leaning close, he whispered in her ear. "I'll do your reading for you. Tell them you forgot your glasses."

She shook her head and whispered back, "It will be all right. You'll see."

Sitting amongst his circle of guests, Dr. Shandler asked, "Who would like to read first?"

Sheridan quickly stood. "I'll go first, Father!" Carefully opening his fragile volume, he said, "This is riddle number sixty-eight, the easiest one. All of you will be able to guess the answer. 'The wave, over the wave, a weird thing I saw, through-wrought, and wonderfully ornate: a wonder on the wave—water became bone.'"

Anthony spoke up. "'Water became bone' must refer to ice."

Sheridan grinned. "An A for Mr. Tidball! Let me try

another. 'I heard of a wonder, of words moth-eaten . . . '"

When Sheridan had finished his riddle of the book-worm, the readings progressed counter-clockwise around the circle. Raymond read next—a selection from *The Faerie Queene* by Edmund Spenser, followed by Serena's interpretation of Thomas Gray's "Ode on the Death of a Favourite Cat." Next, Mrs. Shandler read Sir Francis Bacon's essay, "Of Parents and Children."

Only two others were seated between Isabelle and her hostess—Lon and Tracy. Lon, whose volume contained the works of Robert Burns, chose to read his epitaphs and epigrams. Amusing though they were, Isabelle found herself nervously chewing the inside of her lip in anticipation of her turn.

When Tracy began to read his excerpt from *Beowulf*, near panic set in. Even though he was standing beside her, she couldn't hear him over the cacophony of inner voices screaming of her inadequacies. With a silent prayer, she banished them from mind, clearing her head for what she was about to say.

Tracy closed his book and sat down.

Dr. Shandler said, "And now we will hear Miss Dorlon read an excerpt from Sir Thomas Malory. Go ahead, my dear."

Rising to her feet, she wondered if her knees would buckle. With trembling hands, she opened her book to the first page of text.

CHAPTER

13

Isabelle's voice, though quiet at the start, grew more confident as she spoke.

"'Whan that Aprill with his shoures soote; the droghte of March hath perced to the roote, And hath every veyne in swich licour; Of which vertu engendred is the . . . '"

As the words flowed from her mouth, she could see the curious look on Dr. Shandler's face. When he checked to see which volume he himself was holding, his interruption came as no surprise.

"Pardon me, Miss Dorlon, but those aren't the words of Sir Thomas Malory. They're right here, in the prologue to Chaucer's *Canterbury Tales!*" He pointed to the page in his book.

She closed her own book, offering a feeble smile. "Yes, sir, you're absolutely correct. I was reciting from Chaucer, not Malory."

A tense moment passed, then he chuckled. "Jolly good joke, Miss Dorlon. You were testing us to see if anyone would notice. Jolly good joke, indeed!"

Others murmured agreement.

Isabelle remained standing. When the room grew quiet again, she focused on Dr. Shandler. "My intention was not to play a joke, sir. You see, as hard as I've tried, since I was a very small child I have never been able to . . . " She swallowed hard. Reaching deep within, she mustered the courage to continue, borrowing the words of her mother. " . . . I wasn't blessed with the gift of learning to read."

A stunned silence followed. Even Dr. Shandler, whose glib tongue had ruled the evening, sat speechless. Beside her, Tracy's shoulders slumped, his head bowed. And to her right, Jack's expression was full of pity as his hand reached out to caress hers. Tracy had been shamed. Jack obviously felt tremendously sorry for her. She had let them down and spoiled the evening for everyone else.

Blinded by the tears that sprang unbidden to her eyes, she withdrew from his touch, set the Malory book on her chair, and hurried from the room. Unmindful of where she was going, she found herself in near darkness on the path to the river. Nearly running, she ignored the voices of Jack and her brother calling to her. Aided by the light of a full moon and a sky full of stars, she stepped into one of the canoes, untied it, and pushed off from the dock, paddling upstream.

As she circled the shadowy rock in the bend and started back, her tears began to dry, but within, chaos reigned. Her experiment in honesty had met with dismal failure. She was wondering how she would face Jack and the others again when she heard someone paddling toward her in the other canoe.

"Miss Dorlon! Thank God, I found you!"

She recognized Dr. Shandler's voice, then his silhouette. As he pulled alongside her, she said, "I'm sorry, Dr. Shandler. I'm sorry I—"

Holding their canoes together, he interrupted. "Sorry

for what? A condition you didn't ask for?"

Paying no heed, she continued. "I'm sorry for ruining everyone's evening. I never should have come into the library. Judith warned me—"

"Miss Dorlon, will you *please* let me speak?"

Even in the darkness, she could see his earnest countenance. She held her silence.

He spoke plainly. "You have a disorder. Word blindness. That's why you can't learn to read."

After a moment's contemplation, she said, "I have a disorder? What does that mean? That I'm sick?"

"A disorder is not a disease. Word blindness is different from blood diseases or infectious diseases . . . or even eye diseases," Dr. Shandler patiently explained. "It's not an illness of the flesh. It's just what it says—a blindness to words, a difficulty in the way you perceive them."

Isabelle tried to grasp the full meaning of Dr. Shandler's revelation, saying contemplatively, "Papa couldn't learn to read, either."

"He likely suffered from word blindness, too. It often occurs in more than one member of the same family."

While Isabelle grappled with the meaning of Dr. Shandler's diagnosis, he continued.

"Many people suffer from word blindness. Colleagues of mine over in England discovered the disorder seven years ago and are experimenting with methods of teaching people like you how to read."

Though Isabelle had been listening, she wondered if she'd heard right. "Did you say *many* people suffer from word blindness?"

"Yes. Many people."

The revelation was almost too much to comprehend.

After years of thinking she was the only person on earth who couldn't learn to read, Isabelle had discovered only yesterday that her very own father had been just like her. Now Dr. Shandler was claiming that *many others* suffered the same shame, frustration, and embarrassment where reading was concerned.

He went on. "My colleagues, Dr. Kerr and Dr. Morgan, have discovered that people with word blindness often suffer from more than just the inability to read. Many of them can't learn arithmetic, tell time from a clock, or remember right from left." Pointing to the ribbon on her right wrist, he said, "I'd guess you're one of those."

The accuracy with which Dr. Shandler had described Isabelle's problems convinced her that he was right about this disorder named word blindness. And with her new realization came an immediate question.

"These English doctors, have they found a cure?"

Sadly, he shook his head. "A cure will take time. They're working now to develop a method of teaching people like you how to read. Perhaps one day . . . "

She prayed he was right, that in time, a cure would come. Contemplatively, she finished his sentence, "Perhaps one day I'll be able to walk into your library, pick any book I want from the shelf, and read it to you."

He smiled. "It's entirely possible." His focus shifting to the shore, he said, "Look! We've been talking so long, we've almost drifted home. And some of the others have already come looking for us."

As the boats came alongside the dock, Isabelle saw that Tracy and Jack were there with the others from the library. While her brother tied up Dr. Shandler's canoe, Jack did the same for her, giving her a hand as she stepped out, then guiding her up the path with his palm against her back.

Out of the others' hearing, he told her, "I was ready to come after you in the other canoe when Tracy and Dr. Shandler stopped me. I was so worried about you, it didn't matter whether I could swim or not!"

She looked into his eyes finding no sign of pity now, only concern. "You can stop worrying," she assured him. "I just needed some time alone to think."

Slipping his arm about her waist, he pulled her close. "I'm glad you're all right."

In the shelter of Jack's embrace, and with her new knowledge of word blindness, she told him, "I'm feeling better now than I have in a very long time."

Isabelle was still reflecting on the concept of word blindness the following morning as she accompanied Mrs. Shandler, Serena, and Judith on a shopping trip to Haley's, the city's largest mercantile, where the Shandler women were in search of solid brass-bound trunks, walking shoes, and the latest in millinery for their annual pilgrimage to England to visit paternal family relations. Now, when Isabelle became frustrated over indecipherable signs touting the finer points of merchandise on display, she reminded herself that she had a condition which prevented her from reading those signs.

As interesting as Haley's was, so full of women's furnishings including the very latest of the season—Trouville coat jackets trimmed in Irish lace—Isabelle couldn't help wondering how Jack was doing. Her honesty over her inability to read had given him the courage to make a similar confession regarding his inability to swim which had been met with immediate offers from Tracy, Anthony, and

Sheridan, for a morning lesson in the river.

When Dr. Shandler returned from morning rounds at the hospital and all had gathered in the dining room for luncheon, Anthony said, "Jack has an announcement."

He smiled broadly. Focusing on Isabelle, he told her, "I've learned how to float!"

"That's wonderful!" she replied, secretly wishing her reading problem could be solved so easily.

Sheridan said, "And a mighty fine floater, he is. He could float from here back to Centerport, if he had to!"

Tracy said, "He'll be swimming like a fish before we know it."

The conversation proceeded from swimming, to Serena and her mother's finds at Haley's, to afternoon and evening plans. Anthony, Judith, and the Sheridan women, not being baseball fans, decided to take in a lecture at the Literary Society, for which they were offered the use of the Cadillac. As for the evening, Dr. Shandler had already purchased more than enough tickets for all to attend the locally produced version of the Broadway musical, *Floradora*, being performed at the River Bend Theater.

With ample time to spare before the start of the Robinson-Cartwright game, Dr. Shandler led the others in a procession on foot to the baseball field, choosing seating in the third row midway between home plate and first base.

As Robinson spectators with their brown pennants filled the stands, Jack again recalled for Isabelle how years ago, on a day much like this one, he had watched Erskine trounce Robinson, thus deciding that his future in college ball lay in Centerport, not River Bend.

"The place looks the same today as it did then," he told her, pointing beyond the field to the elms, chestnuts, and maples still bereft of their foliage, and the way they opened to afford a view of the warm red roof of the gymnasium. Farther off, more hardwoods were interspersed with the gabled roofs, turrets, and towers which Jack identified as the academic and residential quadrangles. Turning their attention to matters closer at hand, they agreed that the field, with its stubbly turf and rutted base lines, couldn't compare to Erskine's, thanks to Mr. T's efforts.

As the home team began its warm-up, Isabelle said, "Is it my imagination, or do the Robinson players seem larger than Erskine's?"

Reluctant to grant the point, Jack replied, "I'm not sure." But when the players sat on their bench, their broad shoulders filling it from end to end, he told Isabelle, "You're right, the Robinson nine *are* heavier than the Erskine nine. But the Cartwright players are no bigger than us."

The difference in size led Isabelle to wonder if Cartwright would be overpowered on the field, but during the first seven innings of the game, what the Cartwright team lacked in stature, they made up for in pitching, bringing the score to a 3-3 tie.

A different aspect of Robinson's play concerned Jack, however—their infield. So quick and accurate were they that three times they had made double plays—shortstop-to-second-to-first.

Now, Robinson was at bat again. The first man up, though powerful in his swing, had yet to make a hit in this game. He had connected with the ball once, but had sent it foul of the first base line into the stands a few yards beyond Isabelle, to Jack's right.

When the count stood at one strike and three balls, Jack told Isabelle, "The pitcher's tired. He's losing speed. He'd better be careful, because this batsman will hit hard if he connects."

Isabelle watched intently as the pitcher wound up again. The ball came in fast. The batsman swung. A sharp crack split the air. The drive went foul—straight toward her!

CHAPTER

14

Arms raised, eyes shut, Isabelle waited for the impact of the foul ball.

Jack reached out.

With a loud smack, the rock-hard sphere slapped against his bare palm two inches from her face.

To his left, Dr. Shandler was instantly alarmed. "Miss Dorlon, are you all right?"

Sheridan peered over his father's shoulder. "*Please*, Miss Dorlon, don't be hurt!"

Isabelle opened her eyes and smiled. "Don't worry. I'm fine."

To Jack, Dr. Shandler said, "Let me see your hand."

Palm stinging from the catch, Jack tossed the ball to the waiting player and held his reddened hand out for Dr. Shandler to examine.

After some probing, he said, "Nothing's broken. Ice will help to keep the swelling down."

Sheridan said, "I'll go get some."

Isabelle reached for Jack's injured hand. "I'm so sorry. You'll probably miss several practices and a chance to play in the next game because of me."

Though his palm hurt more with each passing second, her delicate inspection somehow brought comfort. "It wasn't your fault. Besides, better a sore hand than an injured head."

Tracy told Isabelle, "If Weatherby wasn't such a great catch, you'd have been knocked out, for sure." Jostling his teammate's shoulder, he said, "Just because you got a sore hand from protecting my sister, don't expect an easy time of it. Once you've healed, I expect you to work twice as hard—especially after seeing the Robinson infield!"

Jack studied Tracy. "Do you think we could ever be that good?"

Tracy's eyes narrowed. After a moment's thought, he said, "We'd have to practice night and day, but I think we could be better than they are if we stay healthy."

If we stay healthy. Jack pondered the words. First, Perkins, now him. He prayed he'd recover in a few days, and that no one else on the team would suffer injury in practices and games to come.

Sheridan returned with an ice pack obtained from the Robinson trainer and Dr. Shandler pressed it snugly against Jack's palm. Instantly, it began to reduce the pain that was starting to throb. But the doctor's words of advice brought a new sort of discomfort.

"You'll have to take a couple of weeks off from practice in order for that bruise to heal properly."

Jack nodded. In a moment of self-pity he wished he hadn't come to River Bend. Then, gazing at the attractive young lady by his side for whom his fondness was increasing with each passing hour, he realized that he wouldn't have missed this time with her for the world! Or the opportunity to perform as her hero!

Isabelle, having heard Dr. Shandler's words and seeing the solemn expression on Jack's face, felt the blame for his injury even more acutely. Head hanging, she murmured, "I'm sorry, Jack, so sorry."

Reaching with his left hand, he lifted her chin and smiled. "Stop apologizing. Something good will come out of it."

Feeling no less guilty, Isabelle directed her attention to the game once more. The batsman who had nearly hit her, now turned a tired pitcher's delivery into a home run, putting Robinson ahead by one. Then, the Cartwright substitute pitcher came in. But he was nearly as good as the regular and at the end of the ninth inning, the score remained Robinson-4, Cartwright-3.

Climbing down from the stands, she saw a familiar, unfriendly face in the distance. Linking one arm with Jack's and the other with Tracy's, she said, "Let's get out of here. Reginald Billings is headed our way."

But her warning came too late. Within seconds, he was beside Jack, his words as unsavory as his presence. "If it isn't Weatherby, the coward!"

Jack remained silent, summoning all the self-restraint he could muster. A glance at the fire in Tracy's eyes told him the infamous Dorlon temper was ready to flare.

His voice low and threatening, Billings told Jack, "I haven't forgotten what you cost me, Weatherby. Some day, you'll pay with more than a sore hand." His villainous gaze raked Isabelle from head to toe, then he was gone.

Through clenched teeth, Tracy said, "I'm a hair's breadth from taking after him and laying him flat."

Tightening her arm in her brother's, Isabelle said, "Forget it, Tracy. We'll never see him again."

Jack said, "She's right. He's not worth the trouble."

The encounter was forgotten by the time they reached

home. Heading to his aunt and uncle's to eat supper and dress for the musical, Jack promised to meet up with the others at the theater a quarter of an hour before the performance.

Having eaten a light supper of chicken custard, Isabelle retired to the guest suite with Judith to bathe and dress for the theater. Her simple gown of dark blue dotted brilliantine and the unadorned twist in her hair seemed too plain for an evening out, especially compared with the black-lace-over-yellow-taffeta affair Judith was donning, and the fancy, bejeweled bun fastened atop her head. When Serena came knocking on their bedroom door wearing an apricot taffeta gown rich with Irish point lace, and matching silk flowers in her honey-gold hair, Isabelle admitted outright that her own costume and hairstyle seemed completely inadequate.

Heading for the door, Serena said, "I'll be right back. I have just the thing to dress up your gown."

A minute later, she returned with an extraordinarily long strand of pearls and a small wreath of silk rosebuds, lilacs, and leaves for her hair. Looping the pearls into three strands, she slipped them over Isabelle's head and arranged them so that two of the strands wrapped about her neck while the third one hung down, halfway to her knees.

Turning her toward the mirror, Serena asked, "What do you think?"

Isabelle smiled. "Your necklace is a marvelous improvement!"

Pulling out the stool at the vanity, Serena told her, "Have a seat." To Judith, she said, "Of the three of us, you're the hair wizard. Will you please work the flower wreath around Isabelle's twist?"

Judith picked up the wreath, then set it aside again in favor of a hair brush. "With your permission, Isabelle, I'd like to change your twist into a tea-pot-handle bun."

Unsure of the style to which Judith referred, she replied, "I suppose that would be all right."

With only a couple of minutes' effort, Judith brushed out Isabelle's thick, mahogany tresses, fastened some of them into a bun at the back of her head, wrapped the remaining strands around them in a twist, and added to it the flower wreath Serena had brought.

Using a small hand mirror to view the results in the larger one, Isabelle told Judith, "You'll have to teach me how to do that. My hair has never looked so pretty!"

Serena grinned. "Mr. Weatherby won't be able to take his eyes off you!"

Feeling her face grow warm, Isabelle replied, "And my brother won't pay the slightest attention to the musical, the way you look."

"We'll see," Serena said modestly. "*Floradora* is known for its sextet of exceptionally beautiful girls." Opening the door, she said, "It's getting late. We'd better go."

They emerged from the suite at the same time that Tracy and Anthony—who had moved from his accommodations in the dormitory to the guest suite—stepped out of their room across the hall. The way Tracy's gaze lingered on Serena, Isabelle was certain her prediction would prove true—that he wouldn't even notice the girls in the musical. And Anthony was completely taken by the elegant look Judith had achieved in her lace-over-taffeta gown. With the others pairing off, Isabelle was even more eager to be

150

with Jack again. Especially when the only male unspoken for as they left the house was thirteen-year-old Sheridan, and he took it upon himself to escort her to the theater.

He was still serving that role several minutes after they arrived in the lobby. Jack was nowhere to be seen, and Isabelle was growing both worried and annoyed. When the lights dimmed five minutes before the start of the performance, Dr. Shandler handed several tickets to Sheridan.

"Son, take your mother and the others in. I'll stay here and wait for Mr. Weatherby."

A couple of minutes later, when they had settled into the fifth row of the center section, Isabelle turned to look for Jack in hopes that he and Dr. Shandler would be on their way down the aisle to join them. What she saw sent her heart plummeting.

Rather than the silver-haired doctor by Jack's side, a radiant young woman a year or two older than he, had linked her arm with his. And from their expressions as they laughed and conversed with one another, they were more than just friends—they were obviously very fond of one another!

Isabelle wanted to sink into the floor!

How could he show up with someone else when he knew I'd be here waiting for him, she wondered, her cheeks burning. Then a more troubling thought came to her.

How could he be so sweet on that other woman and so nice to me at the same time?

Isabelle felt as though a sword were piercing her heart. The desire to run out of the auditorium overwhelmed her, but it was too late. As the theater went dark for the start of the performance, Mrs. Shandler moved next to her, into the place she had hoped Jack would occupy, leaving the three seats on the aisle for her husband, Jack, and his lady friend.

Though the musical opened with gay songs and dances, and the half-dozen attractive young ladies and escorts for which it had been renowned on Broadway, Isabelle seemed deaf and blind to anything but the vision of the attractive woman at Jack's side. As the minutes dragged by, the pain of betrayal set in, along with the humiliation of playing the fool. Jack had meant more to her than a roomer in her mother's house and a boarder at her table, and she had thought she meant more to him than simply the sister of his teammate and daughter of his landlady.

Obviously, she was mistaken.

Jack had evidently considered Isabelle's friendship one of convenience. With his serious lady friend far away in another city, he undoubtedly had planned from the start to abandon her once he graduated from college and moved on.

For the first time since Isabelle had left Centerport, she wished desperately she were back home. Instead, she had the remainder of a miserable evening to endure. Unable to focus on the dialogue and performances in the musical, she kept thinking of what might have been. Only now, facing the truth that Jack had no place in her future, did she realize how very fond of him she had grown.

Later, when the lights went up for intermission and she watched Jack and his friend ascend the aisle to the lobby, she realized how much more sophisticated the other woman was. Her gown, of pale rose lace adorned with jewels, must certainly have come from either London or Paris. The flounces of Chantilly lace at the bottom of the skirt flowed into a short sweep at the back, complimenting her regal bearing.

But the most impressive aspect of the other woman was revealed when she had arrived with Jack in the lobby. As she turned, Isabelle caught a good look at the woman's face, thoroughly lovely with large, wide-set eyes, a naturally upturned mouth, and a bone structure prominent enough to form a Rembrandt-like hollow in her cheeks. Eager to escape the others' presence, Isabelle had started toward the ladies' lounge when she heard Jack call her name. Pretending not to hear, she continued on her way, staying there until the lights dimmed, warning that the performance was about to resume. Opening the door a couple of inches, she saw that only Jack and a gentleman she recognized as his former neighbor, Judge Whittaker, were in the lobby. Not wanting to spend the remainder of the performance in the lounge, she hurried past Jack.

He called and followed after her, his hand catching her by the elbow, bringing her to a halt. "I was hoping to introduce you to my cousin, but it can wait until after the performance."

Without aforethought, Isabelle asked, "Your *kissing* cousin?"

Jack shook his head, laughing. "My *first* cousin, Catherine. Her new husband was called away on business this weekend so she came home to stay with her folks. She was looking so forlorn, missing him, I invited her to join us for the evening. Dr. Shandler had said he bought too many tickets, and I was hoping the musical would take Catherine's mind off Grady." Jack continued his solemn, careful explanation. "At first, she declined, then she decided to come along. She needed to change her gown. That's why we were so late arriving."

Ashamed that she had doubted him, Isabelle could make no reply.

Seeing that the doors to the auditorium were beginning to close, Jack said, "We'd better find our seats."

Leading her to the fifth row, he was pleased to see that the two places nearest the aisle were waiting for them. Once seated, he wasted no time reaching for her hand, giving it a squeeze, and continuing to hold it tight. Having spent intermission in the counsel of Judith, Serena, Mrs. Shandler, and his cousin, he understood too late the faulty conclusion Isabelle had jumped to. Yet when he had begged the ladies to go to the lounge and explain Catherine's relationship to him, they decided to leave the explaining to him.

And he had suffered greatly in the interim. Longing for Isabelle to know the truth, and equally eager for her to meet the cousin he had admired from his earliest boyhood, he had prayed she would emerge from the lounge with a few minutes to spare before the second half. Now, he would have to wait until the curtain closed. In the meanwhile, he would simply enjoy the pleasure of holding Isabelle's hand in his, and reckon with the new realization that he was more smitten with her than he had previously dared to admit.

With her hand firmly ensconced in Jack's, Isabelle could regret at leisure all the mistaken assumptions she had made about Catherine, who sat immediately to her left. When the curtain closed on the final act, she was ready with an apology, but Jack's cousin was bubbling over with things to say.

"Miss Dorlon, I'm Catherine Baker, Jackie's cousin." She offered her hand. "I'm so thrilled to meet you!"

With reluctance, Isabelle released her hand from Jack's to briefly take Catherine's. "The pleasure is mine." Catherine rushed on. "Jackie barely stopped talking about you from the minute I arrived at Mother and Daddy's till we got to the theater. Usually, he's all baseball, describing in enormous detail every hit and out of every game. Tonight, I had to pry out of him news of the Erskine nine."

Crimson flooding his cheeks, Jack rose and stepped into the aisle. "Catherine, don't you think we'd better go?" He indicated the others vacating the auditorium.

Rising slowly, Catherine continued to focus on Isabelle. "Jackie was so insistent on telling me about you, he barely gave me time to dress for the musical. He says you're a first-rate swimmer, a highly skilled broom maker, well-versed in literature, and that you're the prettiest young woman he's ever seen!"

"Is that so?" Isabelle replied in amazement.

"It's true, every word," Catherine affirmed. Linking her arm with Isabelle's, she walked her toward the exit. "In fact, Jackie is so fond of you, I told him I was afraid he'd be down the aisle and making a start on his own family of little ball players before he even had his sheepskin in hand!"

Left speechless by Catherine's last statement, Isabelle was glad to reach the lobby where Dr. Shandler began introducing Jack's cousin to the others in their company. Acquaintances made, he asked, "Would you and Mr. Weatherby please join us for dessert at the Michigan Street Inn, my treat? I'm sure you're acquainted with their famous five-layer fudge cakes and their creamy vanilla custards."

Giving Jack no choice, Catherine answered, "We'd be

155

pleased to join you!"

At the inn, Catherine's naturally chatty ways made her the dominant participant in conversation, though Isabelle never found her boring or self-centered. Her stories of a honeymoon trip to Europe and journeys with Grady to California for his business proved fascinating. Jack seemed quieter than usual, but Isabelle couldn't blame him after the way Catherine had carried on about him in the auditorium.

Before the evening ended, Judith extended an invitation to Jack to travel in her father's private car on the trip home. He accepted, although reluctantly, it seemed. When he and Catherine parted to return to her folks' place, he barely bid Isabelle good night.

The moment she reached the guest suite at Shandlers, Judith and Serena were all a twitter about Catherine's statements regarding Jack's fondness for her.

Unhooking the bodice of her black lace gown, Judith said, "Jack's so sweet on you, Isabelle, he'll probably melt in the next rain storm!"

Plucking an apricot silk flower from her hair, Serena added, "Evidently his heart has been melting for some time now. I'd say your days as Miss Dorlon are numbered!"

Uncomfortable with such talk, Isabelle removed Serena's pearls and hair ornament, placed them in her hands, and pointed her toward the door. "Thank you very much for loaning me these. It's been a long evening and I need my rest. See you in the morning!"

Taking the hint, Serena let herself out and closed the door behind her, only to open it again an instant later with the words, "Good night, future Mrs. Weatherby! Pleasant dreams!"

Isabelle reached for a pillow, but Serena was gone

before she could throw it. Evidently judging silence to be the wisest course, Judith quietly climbed into bed.

Turning out the light, Isabelle lay awake staring into the darkness, wondering to what degree Catherine's statements about Jack's feelings had been true. The possibility that he cared about her as much as Catherine claimed thrilled her to her very depths. It scared her, too. She hadn't thought about friendship turning into marriage, or fondness evolving into a love strong enough to last a lifetime. She prayed that God would guide both her and Jack in matters of the heart.

The following morning, on the trip home, Jack remained quiet and aloof, sitting off by himself to read and study, so he told Isabelle. But deep inside, he was suffering anxiety over Catherine's too-honest revelations about his feelings for that certain miss.

Isabelle was fully aware of the reserved nature that had come over Jack. She was confident that whatever was bothering him, he would discuss it with her when he was ready. In the meantime, she turned her attention to Tracy who was also trying to catch up on assignments for Monday classes. She tried to concentrate on the words of Shelley as her brother softly read "Ode to the West Wind" from his English Literature text, but her mind kept wandering. She was glad when they finally pulled into the Centerport depot.

A trio of Anthony's supporters met him, carting him triumphantly down the platform on their shoulders. Released from his admirers, he returned to Judith who was in front of the station arranging with the freight hauler for bags to be delivered to the proper addresses.

Seeing Mr. Jamison's Cadillac and knowing its capacity was too limited to carry all of Judith's guests, Jack and Tracy started walking home. Isabelle had already joined them when she saw Coach Hanson coming their way, newspaper beneath his arm, frown firmly in place.

Tracy greeted him cheerfully. "Coach, we got a good look at the Robinson team. They're tough, but if we work extra hard, we can beat them when we go to River Bend in June."

Hanson's scowl deepened. "If we don't do something quick, there isn't going to be any game at Robinson." Unfolding the *Erskine College Journal*, he pointed to a headline. "Look at this."

Tracy read out loud. "'Baseball Team Low on Funds. Season in Jeopardy.'"

Jack's heart skipped a beat. "How can that be?"

Hanson sighed. "The article claims the Athletic Committee is short on funds. If we don't come up with six hundred dollars, our season is over with the home game against Sutherland on the second of May!"

With a sick feeling deep inside his gut, Jack saw his baseball career at Erskine—the dream of his lifetime—ending abruptly before it had properly begun.

CHAPTER

15

Isabelle listened intently as Hanson summarized the article.

"The rotten weather we had last fall cut the football receipts in half. That left the Athletic Committee short on funds for baseball. We've got enough to travel to one more away game, then we're done—unless we can raise money the way Dean Levatt thinks we can."

Tracy asked, "And how's that?"

Skepticism prominent on his brow, Hanson replied, "By popular subscription. He's calling a mass meeting this Tuesday. He wants you and me to sell everyone on the idea of contributing out of their own pockets to keep the team playing."

"I can't do that!" Tracy argued. "I'm no good at speech-making!"

Hanson sighed. "Neither am I."

Seeing Jamisons' Cadillac approaching, an idea came to Isabelle. She waved it to a halt, her focus on Anthony. "Mr. Tidball, the Erskine nine urgently need to enlist your services for a speech!"

Anthony laughed. "Me? Give a speech about baseball? I've never even played the game!"

Jack asked, "Have you ever watched the Erskine nine play?"

Anthony shook his head. "I don't know much about

the subject, except what I've picked up from listening to you fellows at mealtime."

Tracy told Isabelle, "I hate to criticize, but I think you're making a big mistake, asking Anthony to speak on a sport he knows nothing about."

Isabelle ignored his doubt. "Anthony's speech wouldn't be about the game. It would be about loyalty to the school and supporting the team so they can go to River Bend and defeat Robinson the way Anthony and his debate team did."

Anthony said, "I don't think the team needs me to stir up enthusiasm for them."

Hanson spoke up. "We need more than enthusiasm, Mr. Tidball. We need money. The team is nearly broke."

"But—"

Opening the paper, Hanson cut him off. "'To obliterate the stigma of last year's defeat by Robinson is what every friend of the college hopes for and expects. But unless enough money is placed at the disposal of the management to meet the expenses of the team, such a victory cannot be secured.'" Focusing on Anthony, he said, "There's going to be a mass meeting Tuesday evening to solicit contributions, otherwise, the season ends on the second of May. You're a friend of the college—of the team, aren't you?"

"Yes, but—"

"All Miss Dorlon is asking is that you give a speech Tuesday night."

Isabelle said, "You can do that much, Anthony. You can convince the students to part with some money for a cause as worthy as the Erskine nine."

Smiling ruefully, Anthony argued, "I'm afraid my inexpertise could hurt more than help."

160

Judith countered. "Your greatest skill is in persuading people."

Jack said, "The fact that you're not on the team makes you an unprejudiced spokesperson. It would stand in your favor."

Judith said, "Mr. Weatherby is right. You're the perfect candidate for the speech."

Tracy said, "Judith, Isabelle, Jack, you've convinced me." He told Anthony, "They're right. You *should* make the speech."

After a long, thoughtful moment, Anthony drew a deep breath. "All right. I'll do it. But don't expect me to sound like I did when I was talking about the automobile."

Hanson smiled. "Thanks, Tidball!"

As the Cadillac chugged away on down the street, Isabelle prayed Anthony's speech would produce the necessary results, and that Tracy and Jack would be allowed to play out the season to the finish.

Minutes later, when she approached home, thoughts of baseball vanished when she realized her mother was sitting on a recently painted front porch. Above it, the roof had been repaired with new shingles, and the eaves cleaned of winter debris.

Her mother rose, her arms spread in welcome. "How was your trip?"

"Wonderful!" Isabelle replied, returning the hug.

Tracy kissed his mother's cheek. Indicating the paint job on the porch, he said, "Someone's been busy since we left for River Bend."

Tilda beamed. "Mr. Herder—Mr. Jamison's hired man, don't you know. He showed up Saturday morning and insisted his boss would have his hide if he didn't freshen up our porch by the time Jamisons came back from Detroit."

Inside, Chips began barking loudly.

Reaching for the door handle, Jack told Isabelle, "Someone's eager for a walk, now that you're home again."

She smiled. "You'll join us, won't you?"

He shook his head. "I still have lots of studying to do before classes tomorrow."

Isabelle entered the front door to be slobbered by kisses from her beloved mutt. As she passed the stairs on her way to fetch his leash, she couldn't help noticing the slump in Jack's shoulders when he ascended to his room. Evidently, the financial woes of the Erskine nine were taking a heavy toll.

Two days later, from his desk by the back window, Jack gazed out on the shed where Isabelle was working. Ever since his return from River Bend he had tried to immerse himself in studies and baseball to avoid thinking about her. But his plan failed miserably. Each evening when she invited him to walk with her and Chips, he longed to accept. Only with great self-discipline did he manage to decline her invitations and remain in his room, supposedly studying. But his mind often wandered from the ancient history of Rome or complex problems in trigonometry to the young woman in the work shed. The more he pondered his feelings for Isabelle, the more he realized Catherine's assessment of the situation was right. He had found the one with whom he wanted to spend the rest of his life, and the fact that she had not yet mastered the ability to read did nothing to diminish his desire for her.

But his college degree must come first. A year and more separated him from his diploma. It seemed a lifetime away. Even so, when the opportunity presented itself, he would share his feelings with her.

He shoved his history text aside, and with it thoughts of Isabelle. The difficulties of financing the baseball team foremost on his mind, the time had arrived to head over to the mass meeting. As he approached the auditorium, he prayed a good crowd would turn out, and that they would be generous in their response. But a while later, when Dean Lavatt had concluded ten minutes of uninspired remarks, Jack grew concerned. Even from his front row seat amongst the Erskine nine and substitutes, he sensed the uneasiness at the back of the hall. Fellows behind him were scraping their feet. Several walked out before Anthony had even taken the podium. Once he did, Jack and Tracy led an enthusiastic round of applause which was amplified by a cry of "A—a—ay, Tidball!" from Lon and Raymond.

Anthony settled his spectacles on his nose, shuffled his papers, and offered a nod of acknowledgement which was met with more cheers, clapping, and stomping of feet. Fellows edging toward the door turned back and settled into their seats again. The tumult died down and Anthony began to speak.

"I'll tell you frankly that I know nothing about baseball."

A freshman booed, instantly hushed by two seniors.

Anthony continued. "I've seen but one game. I guess that's why I'm not able to understand the science of hitting a ball with a wagon spoke and running over salt bags."

Hanson laughed heartily. Jack joined in, then Tracy and the others on the team, but their forced joviality failed to engage the audience.

Anthony said, "Your captain, Tracy Dorlon, tells me that down at Robinson they've found an old wagon wheel, cut the fingers off a pair of kid gloves, bought a wire bird cage, and started a baseball club. He says that last year, that club beat his. This year, his club wants to even the score. Trouble is, his club hasn't any money. If it doesn't get some money his team won't have the railway fare to go to River Bend and put Robinson in its place.

"What's to be done? Are we to stand idly by with our hands in our pockets and see Robinson walk off with a game that rightfully belongs to us? Or are we to take our hands out of our pockets and jingle some coins into the collection box?"

In the absolute silence that followed, Jack prayed that the speech would end with enough jingling of coins to keep his baseball dream alive.

Anthony resumed his speech. "Even though I'm not a baseball enthusiast, I *am* an Erskine enthusiast. We can't beat Robinson in baseball unless we show up for the game. The sum of six hundred dollars is needed."

Grumbling could be heard in the center section.

Anthony pointed to the offender. "You, in the green shirt. If you don't think victory over Robinson is worth six hundred dollars, stand up and walk out."

Echoes of, "Yeah! Stand up and walk out!" rippled through the auditorium.

The grumbler, eyes downcast, sank low in his seat.

Still focused on him, Anthony said, "All right, then. I challenge you and everyone else to contribute your fair share to the collection box. The team needs on average, one dollar from each person here."

Whispers stirred.

"To some of you, that may sound like a lot, but to others, it's just pocket change. Now, before I step down, I'd like to lead three cheers for the nine. Hip-hip—"

Lon and Raymond sprang to their feet with, "Hooray!"

On the next cheer, half the fellows lent their voices, and by the final round, the hall thundered with cheers and applause.

Tracy and five other regulars took up posts at the ends of the rows, passing three boxes amongst the right, center, and left sections of the auditorium, starting at the back. Jack prayed for generous giving, tossing a silver dollar in the box when his turn came. But as he passed it to the player beside him, he thought it weighed far too little to represent a third of the total receipts needed.

When the auditorium had emptied of all but Anthony, the players, and their coach, Hanson pulled the curtains on stage and gathered everyone around a table in the wing. Setting the three boxes in front of him, he said, "Let's open 'em up and see what we've got."

Jack watched as the coins and folding money were separated from slips of paper on which some fellows had written pledges of support. Then the counting began, and tiny stacks representing ten dollars apiece dotted the table. A few minutes later, Coach Hanson tallied the number of stacks.

" . . . twenty-six, twenty-seven, twenty-eight, twenty-nine and," he counted the last few remaining coins, adding a quarter from his own pocket. "Three hundred dollars even." With a deep sigh, he said, "That's enough to see us through till the end of the month, but it'll be a short season unless you fellows have an idea how to raise another three hundred dollars."

165

Silence ensued.

Jack's heart sank. His long-held dream of winning in River Bend against Robinson was now a fading fancy.

From the back of the auditorium came firm footsteps, then a confident male voice.

"Mr. Tidball? Are you there?"

"Back here, Mr. Jamison!" Anthony pulled aside the heavy gold curtain.

Mounting the stage, Mr. Jamison stepped into the wing. His gaze took in the entire company, then settled on Anthony. "I can see from the glum faces that you've come up short."

"Yes, sir. The team needs another three hundred dollars to finish the season with a win at Robinson."

Jamison pulled a fat money clip from his pocket and began counting. Peeling off several bills, he focused on Tracy.

"Captain, I have a hundred and fifty dollars in my hand. I'm going to give it to your coach in trust. If you ball players can raise a like amount, it's yours. Otherwise, you forfeit my contribution, and the last away games of your season.

"Thank you, sir! We won't forfeit!"

Jack led a chorus of thanks from the others.

With a nod, Jamison draped his thick arm over Anthony's slim shoulders and began escorting him off the stage with the words, "Mr. Tidball, I have a business proposition for you . . . "

Alone with his coach and teammates again, Tracy asked, "Anybody know how we can raise a hundred and fifty dollars before the second week of May?"

After a moment's consideration, Jack said, "I do."

CHAPTER

16

Hurrying home ahead of Tracy and Gregory, Jack was pleased to see that the light was still on in the work shed. Going straight to the door, he knocked soundly.

Inside, Chips let out warning barks, quieting down when he recognized Jack's voice.

"Isabelle, it's me, Jack. May I please talk to you?"

Quickly, she doused her light and stepped outside, asking eagerly, "Did the team get the funds it needs to finish the season?"

He shook his head. "We're still short."

"Then how will you get to River—"

He pressed a finger to her lips. "I'll explain later. Right now, there's something more important on my mind." Reaching for her hand, he said, "Isabelle, I'm sorry I've seemed so aloof these past couple of days."

The warmth of his touch coupled with his humble words sent a warmth through her. "That's all right. You've had a lot on your mind."

"It's not all right," he insisted. "A while back, when you behaved the same way, I made you promise never to do it again. Now, I'm guilty of that very offense, and I apologize."

She squeezed his hand. "Apology accepted."

"Thank you." Leading her toward the back door, he

said, "Listen, I've got to make a quick trip to the Western Union office. I thought maybe you and Chips would keep me company."

"Certainly! But to whom are you sending a telegram, if I may ask?"

"Remember the question you started to ask me a minute ago?"

She nodded.

"Why don't you fetch Chips's leash and I'll tell you the answer on the way."

When the threesome were headed down Elm toward Main Street, Jack said, "I'm wiring Judge Whittaker. He said that if ever I needed anything, to let him know, and I certainly have a need—along with the rest of the team—to get to River Bend in June." He explained about the Jamison challenge and his hope that perhaps Judge Whittaker would also contribute $150.

When he had sent the wire, he suggested a route home through the park. Pausing at Isabelle's favorite bench, he invited her to sit, taking a place close beside her.

While crickets and tree frogs filled the balmy night air with their soft lullaby, Jack gazed at the pretty woman beside him. Warmed by a contentment that came only with her nearness, he took both her hands in his, struggling for the words to convey his feelings.

Even in the pale beams of the gas lantern, Isabelle could see the faint lines that had formed between Jack's brows. She prayed that Judge Whittaker would come through so he and the others on the team could stop worrying. As her silent plea went up, Jack began to speak, but his words were not about baseball or money.

"Isabelle, ever since Saturday night, I've been haunted

by the things my cousin Catherine said about us."

Prepared for a denial that his feelings for her exceeded friendship, Isabelle tried to withdraw her hands from his, but he held tight and continued.

"I know now why they bothered me so. It's because they're true."

Certain her ears were playing tricks, Isabelle spoke tentatively. "It's because . . . they're true?"

Jack nodded. "I care a great deal for you, Isabelle." Raising her hands to his lips, he pressed a kiss on each of them. "I want to be with you, always."

Her senses thrilled to his touch while her heart rejoiced at his words. Yet doubts lingered, fueled by the one short-coming she struggled with daily. "Always is a long, long time," she cautioned.

His mouth turned upward. "Not long enough, considering the way I feel about you." Drawing a shallow breath, he said, "Isabelle, I'd ask you to promise yourself to me this very night, if I didn't have another year of schooling ahead of me."

"Promise myself to you?" she echoed faintly. "Jack, I care for you deeply, but . . . have you forgotten? I don't know how to read, and I might never learn."

He tightened his hold of her. "That's not important. What's important is the way I feel about you. I . . . I love you, Isabelle Dorlon!"

The words she thought would bring only joy, now brought the pain of guilt and a shadow of fear. "Jack, I care for you more than . . . " Unable to find a suitable comparison, she lowered her gaze from his intent, posses-sive look, to the large, strong hands enclosing hers. Her throat constricting with emotion, she whispered, "There's a good chance that, if I ever have children, they won't be able to read, either."

He pulled her close, into the circle of his arms, kissing away the tear that slid down her cheek. "I don't care if they can't read. I'll love them anyway, just because they're yours."

Overflowing with happiness, she dabbed away her tears with the handkerchief he offered, then met his tender gaze with her own. "Jack, I love you, and I would promise myself to you tonight, if you were to but ask. I don't mind that you have another year of school to finish!"

Again, he told her he loved her, hugging her so hard, for a moment she couldn't breathe. Then, his arm snugly about her waist, he walked her home.

Two days later, as the Erskine nine and their substitutes gathered in the locker room after practice to grapple with the money problem again, Jack opened the reply he'd received by special delivery from the judge only an hour ago. Although it didn't contain precisely the answer he'd been hoping for, it did offer a reasonable solution to the deficit problem. He read out loud.

"'Dear Jack,

"'Regarding your need for funding, I propose that you hold a drawing for my 1901 Oldsmobile following your home game against Sutherland on the second of May. In that regard, I have several suggestions for enhancing your revenues, increasing attendance at the game, and disarming objections to games of chance which one always encounters in endeavors of this nature.

"'First, ask your local printer to donate his services in making up special tickets for the game. All ticket holders

170

for this game will become eligible to win the 1901 Oldsmobile.

"'Have your printer design the tickets so there is a purchase price of fifty cents printed on them, a number showing on each end, and a place for the purchaser to write his name and address. This portion of the ticket will be entered in the drawing leaving a stub with the identical number in the hands of the customer.

"'Ask your printer also to donate posters advertising the drawing. Include the enclosed cut of the 1901 Oldsmobile and slogans on the posters, and state that tickets for the game may be purchased in advance from team members, general store merchants, or at the gate. State also that the winner need not be present.

"'Plaster Centerport with the posters and supply each of the general merchants in Lakeshore County with a poster and several tickets. Offer the store owners five cents for each ticket sold as an incentive. Send posters to newspaper editors in your region as well. And please send me ten posters and three hundred tickets, for I am certain I will have no difficulty distributing them amongst my friends and business associates.

"'When your game is over, have the captain of the Sutherland team come to the center of the field to draw the winning ticket from a basket.

"'By now, your receipts should be well in excess of the $650 you will reimburse me for my automobile. Any amount above that is yours for team expenses!

"'One last thing. Let me know as quickly as possible whether you wish to proceed with the plan so I can ship the Oldsmobile to you at my own expense. When it arrives in Centerport, put it on display in the busiest part of town, perhaps in front of the general merchandise store. Leave it there during the days preceding the game, then move it to the field just before you play against Sutherland.

"'My best to you and your teammates with this or any other plan you may have for obtaining sufficient funding to meet your expenses.

"'Sincerest regards, Judge Whittaker.'"

Jack handed the letter to Coach Hanson and took a seat on the bench between Tracy and Gregory.

The coach glanced at it briefly, then focused on his players. "Any discussion?"

King, the pitcher who had replaced Billings, said, "Sounds like a lot of work—distributing posters, selling tickets."

Knox, the shortstop, said, "But look at the money we could make! We could probably sell two thousand tickets!"

Lowe, the left fielder, said, "You think so? At fifty cents apiece, we'll be lucky to unload half that amount. Then what'll we do for the other $150 we'll owe the judge for his car?"

Motter, the third baseman, said, "Yeah. It's too risky. Besides, there's a whole lot of folks who wouldn't give a plug nickel for a motor car, much less a half-dollar for a *chance* on one."

Three others mumbled agreement.

Jack stood again. "You fellows were there the night Mr. Jamison's Cadillac came in on the train. The whole town turned out to see it. Folks are keen on automobiles, and any number of them would probably give a dollar for two chances to own one!"

Motter said, "I didn't see you that night, Weatherby!"

Lowe said, "Yeah, if you're so keen on them, why

weren't you there?"

When further grumbling had died down, Jack replied, "Automobiles are no novelty to me. I spent two years living next door to Judge Whittaker's Oldsmobile. He gave me all the rides I wanted in it—even taught me how to drive."

King spoke again. "I still say it sounds like too much work, selling tickets and all."

Tracy stood, his cheeks red. "You're a bunch of lazy bums! The only thing you seem to care about is being on the field playing ball. Well, it's not that simple. If you want to beat Robinson this year, you've got to *earn* your way to River Bend!"

Stiles rose to speak. "Tracy's right! We've got to work just as hard *off* the field as we do *on* it. Maybe we can't sell two thousand tickets to that game, but if we really try, we can sell enough to pay the judge for his car, and meet the Jamison challenge."

Lowe got to his feet. "If the Judge is willing to pay freight and sell three hundred tickets, seems to me we ought to be able to do the rest."

Northup sprang to his feet. "Lowe is right! I say we go ahead!"

Bissell, the center fielder, said, "Put it to a vote!"

Coach Hanson said, "If there's no more discussion, we'll take a vote."

When those standing had returned to the bench, he continued. "All those in favor, raise your right hand."

Immediately, Tracy, Jack, Stiles, Knox, Lowe, and Northup raised their hands. A moment later, Bissell did the same.

Coach Hanson said, "Seven to six, the vote carries.

Jack, wire Judge Whittaker to ship his Oldsmobile right away. Tracy, stop in at the *Centerport Daily* office on your way home and ask if they'll donate printing services. Stiles, talk to Mr. Reilly and see if he'll let us park the Oldsmobile in front of his store and sell tickets. See you all tomorrow at the game."

For Jack, even though he sat out Friday afternoon's game against Mid-State College, the Erskine win by one run was a welcome prelude to the arrival of Judge Whittaker's Oldsmobile that evening at the depot. Early the following morning, he drove it to the *Centerport Daily* office to pick up the posters and tickets being donated to the cause. Leaving half of them for Tracy and the other team members to distribute and sell around town, he packed the others beneath a tarp behind the seat of the Curved-Dash Olds alongside some of Isabelle's brooms. With a disappointed Chips left behind due to lack of space, he and Isabelle set out for Gerrydale, the first of many stops around the county.

A crowd gathered the minute they came to a halt outside the Gerrydale General Store, and for the first time, Isabelle saw a side to Jack that was neither quiet nor reserved. With great enthusiasm he described the automobile's finer points, focusing on a gentleman in a top hat who was giving the Olds a good looking-over.

"She has a single-cylinder, four-stroke engine." A sweep of his hand indicated the power plant beneath the seat. "She can produce seven horsepower at five hundred revolutions per minute. In addition, she has an all-spur geared two-speed transmission, center chain drive, and two longitudinal springs running fore and aft which serve as

174

side frame members." More gestures indicated their locations.

As he spoke, Jack noticed that the county sheriff was approaching on his mount. Paying him no mind, he continued.

"This is the most delectable little car as ever has been built—the best thing on wheels! She gives one chug per telegraph pole. When you're in an Oldsmobile, you have nothing to watch but the road!" He pulled tickets from his pocket. "And you can own this sweet little motor machine—if you buy a ticket to the Erskine College baseball game and your name is drawn as the winner. Just fifty cents a ticket!"

The hefty sheriff dismounted, his gruff demand directed at Jack. "What's goin' on here?"

Meeting his cross look with a smile, Jack read the lawman's name off his badge. "Good morning, Sheriff Brogan! I'm Jack Weatherby of the Erskine College baseball team. We've come up a little short of funds to finish our season's schedule, so we've decided to raise extra money by holding a drawing. A mere fifty cents could put you behind the tiller of this exquisite mechanical device. Why, in a day's time, she'll take you over a hundred miles of county roads, rather than just the twelve you're going on that gelding of yours . . . fine horse though he is."

Skepticism marked the sheriff's countenance. "Baseball team, eh?"

"Yes, sir!" Jack promptly retrieved a poster from the storage compartment for him to read.

Meanwhile, the gentleman in the top hat pulled two dollars from his pocket. "I've never attended a baseball game, but I'll take four tickets."

"Yes, sir!" Jack quickly counted them out, then continued his explanation. "You need not be present to win. Be sure to fill in your name and address, then give that portion of the ticket to me to enter in the drawing if you don't plan to attend the game. If your name is drawn, we'll deliver this little buggy right to your door!"

Several others came forward to purchase tickets.

Jack was in the midst of making transactions with Isabelle's assistance when the sheriff handed back the poster.

"Care to purchase a ticket, sheriff? The money goes to a good cause," Jack reminded him.

The sheriff shook his head. "You just watch yourself in that thing. Keep your speed down to ten miles an hour," he warned, "or I'll put you under arrest."

"Yes, sir! You won't catch me speeding," Jack promised.

When he had finished business in front of the Gerrydale General Store, he saw that a rather paunchy fellow in an apron was looking on from the front steps. Isabelle introduced him as the proprietor, Mr. Carter, to whom she explained the nature of the ticket sales, promising that she would come to pick up the filled-out entries, unsold tickets, and proceeds minus the shopkeeper's ten percent on the day before the game.

Placing a poster prominently in the front window, Mr. Carter told her and Jack, "If you'll leave me twenty tickets, I'm pretty sure I can sell them 'tween now and the second of May."

Jack smiled broadly. "Glad to oblige, sir!"

While he counted out the tickets and wrote up a receipt,

Isabelle checked on Mr. Carter's inventory of brooms. Finding several sold, she replaced them with new ones carrying the *I. Dorlon* name.

She shuddered when Mr. Carter inspected the handle of a hearth broom, commenting, "I see a different initial on the broom handle this time."

Reluctantly, she admitted, "I've been making the Dorlon brooms since papa died. My brother insisted it was time to tell the truth, and to put my own name on them."

Mr. Carter's face lit up. "I knew something was different about your brooms. All this time, I just figured your brother was a natural at broom making. No offense to your papa, may he rest in peace, but did you know, Miss Dorlon, that you make a *better* broom than he ever did?"

Her face growing warm, she managed a modest, "Thank you, Mr. Carter. I'm glad you're satisfied with my work."

Finished at the general merchandise, they left a poster with the editor of the village newspaper, all the while under the surveillance of the sheriff, who followed them to Horseshoe Harbor. Careful to keep within the speed limit, Jack drove to Krump's Corners, Larches, Vyderland, Jenningsville, Bunson Town, Nichol City, and Dramerton, tailed all the way by the lawman.

Isabelle was amazed that, even at the conservative speed necessitated by county law, she could visit three times more towns in a day than she could driving the buckboard. When she arrived home with Jack at half past five, they were totally depleted of brooms, posters, and tickets. Chips hurried out to meet them the moment the Oldsmobile chugged into the driveway.

Tracy followed, a scowl firmly in place. "Weatherby,

I'm really beginning to wonder about this idea of yours to hold a drawing for an automobile." He kicked the tire in seeming frustration. "The fellows and I have been out all day long trying to sell those tickets, and how many do you think we sold?"

Jack remained mute, praying silently that his plan wouldn't prove a failure as Tracy implied.

CHAPTER

17

Jack's eyes narrowed. "I . . . I don't know, Tracy. How many tickets did you sell?"

"Awe, come on, Weatherby, take a guess," Tracy insisted crossly.

"Two dozen? A dozen? I really don't have any idea."

Exchanging his frown for a smile that stretched the limits of his jaw, Tracy said, "Two hundred and ten! We took in a hundred and five dollars!"

Jack drew a deep breath. "That's terrific! We—"

Isabelle cut him off. "How many tickets do you think *we* sold, brother dear?"

"A hundred."

She shook her head.

"A hundred and fifty?"

Jack spoke up. "You'll have to go much higher than that."

"Two hundred?" Tracy asked.

Isabelle and Jack shook their heads.

"Not more than two hundred," Tracy said in disbelief.

Isabelle and Jack simply grinned.

Tracy scratched his jaw. "Two hundred and ten? That would be another hundred and five dollars."

Jack said, "Add a double sawbuck to that amount."

"You made a hundred and twenty-five dollars? I don't believe it!"

Isabelle lifted the corner of the tarp in the storage compartment behind her, retrieved two small white bundles, and handed them to her brother. "Count it for yourself!"

Feeling the weight of Jack's and his sister's handkerchieves which had been drawn up at the corners and tied into knots, he said, "Wait till Coach Hanson hears the news!"

Jack said, "Climb in. We'll do more than tell him. We'll *show* him."

Settling into the cargo area, Tracy said, "Afterward, we'd better park this little machine in front of Reilly's and walk home. The sooner it goes on display, the better."

Several days later, Jack lingered at the field after practice, sitting alone on the bench to gaze out at the ball diamond where he would play in tomorrow's match against Arundel. It would be his first game since his hand had healed. Unable to take exercise on the field, he had spent hours at the lagoon. And while he was pleased that he had made progress with his swimming, he was eager to return to baseball. He prayed he and his teammates would make a good showing.

He prayed, too, that the Erskine nine would succeed in raising the funds necessary to take them to River Bend in June. While he was laid up with his hand, he'd spent an extraordinary amount of time at Reilly's General Merchandise hawking tickets on the Oldsmobile, but sales had been slow since the day he and Isabelle drove around the county. He was trying to think of ways to boost sales when Mr. T came shuffling down the third base line, pausing to sit beside him on the bench. The old fellow's grin, and his lighthearted words made a welcome diversion from financial worries.

"A penny for y'r thoughts, Weatherby."

Jack smiled. "How about fifty cents? That'll buy you another chance on the Oldsmobile."

The old fellow registered surprise. "*Another* chance? I haven't got my first one, yet."

"Why not? You're eligible to win. It's just the team members and Coach Hanson and their families who aren't supposed to enter the drawing."

Mr. T lowered his gaze, studying a callous on his thumb. When he made no reply, Jack drew his own conclusion.

"I'd forgotten. You don't care much for automobiles."

The old fellow shook his head. "That ain't it. I think it would be mighty interestin', ownin' a motor machine." He chuckled. "After all, if I didn't like it, I could always sell it!"

Knowing Mr. T's special fondness for the Erskine nine, Jack grew increasingly curious as to why he hadn't supported their fund-raising effort. He was still trying to puzzle it out when the old man spoke again.

"Weatherby, I've given plenty of thought to buyin' a chance or two on Judge Whittaker's Oldsmobile. Plain truth of it is . . . I just can't afford it right now."

"But I thought the school paid you—"

"I make a fair wage here at Erskine. Don't get me wrong," Mr. T hastily assured him. A thoughtful moment later, he added, "Truth is, I been helpin' fellas on the team with schoolin' expenses over the years. Right now, I just

181

ain't got the extra for a chance on that Oldsmobile."

Mr. T explained how he and his wife had decided years ago after learning they would never have children of their own, to help young men in need of financial assistance. Though his wife had long since passed away, Mr. T carried on the custom, moving into simple college housing near the athletic fields after her death so he could afford to help even more students.

As Jack headed for home, he pondered Mr. T's self-lessness, and later that evening, when he had returned to his room to begin his studies, he took two quarters from his pocket, an unsold ticket from the hundreds that remained, and wrote Mr. T's name on it.

Days later, in the locker room before the start of the game against Sutherland, Jack listened to the rumblings of the storm that had moved in off the lake an hour earlier. Pulling on his purple stockings and working the laces of his shoes tighter, he prayed the rain would abate soon so as not to detract from gate receipts or—worse yet—force a postponement of the game. Even though advance ticket sales had already put $300 in the team's coffers, a minimum of $500 more was needed to pay Judge Whittaker for the Oldsmobile and to match the Jamison challenge. Jack prayed the team would not fall short. He prayed, too, for his teammates to play with steady hands and nerves.

Joe Perkins limped over and clapped him on the shoulder encouragingly.

"I know you'll do fine out there, Weatherby. You and Tracy and Knox gave a great showing against Arundel on Tuesday." He referred to a double play they'd made, shortstop to first to second, in a game that had ended in a two-to-one victory for Erskine.

"Thanks, Joe. I'll do my best," Jack promised.

Considering the hard work his team had put in—longer hours of practice for the nine, extra workout sessions for Tracy, Knox, and himself since the recovery from his hand injury, and a rotating shift of players stationed in front of Reilly's during store hours to sell tickets, it couldn't come to naught. He prayed again.

Interrupted by the creak of the locker room door, he looked up to find Mr. T enrobed in rain gear which was dripping profusely onto the tile floor.

The attention of the entire team turned to the grounds-keeper and their coach as Hanson approached the older man.

"What do you think, Mr. T? How's the field?"

Tuttle wiped moisture from his crevassed face with the back of his hand. "Good thing that dry spell come when it did. The field needed a good soakin'. We'll be all right for another hour or so, providin' it don't come down any harder than it is right now."

A crack of thunder sent Jack into prayer once more as the elderly man departed.

Though only five minutes remained until the scheduled start of the game, Isabelle made no effort to leave the front parlor where she was watching the rain fall steadily on the brick street. Chips wandered in and sat down beside her, leaning against her skirt and nuzzling her idle hand. Mindlessly stroking his ear, she prayed even as the rain swelled the puddles on the front walk.

"Lord, *please* send your winds to blow this storm away. The fellows have worked so hard to prepare for this game.

You've given them success against Arundel, now let them have a good crowd at the field, and a victorious nine innings!"

Her mother's voice joined hers, saying, "Amen!" Crossing the room, Tilda rested her arm about Isabelle's waist, watching and listening as raindrops continued in rhythm against the roof. A minute or so later, Isabelle's mother pulled back the lacy curtain to study the clouds.

"The sky is brightening to the west. This storm is about rained out," she stated confidently.

As if in disagreement, thunder cracked overhead.

Isabelle sighed. "Wishful thinking."

Saying no more, her mother left the parlor. Isabelle heard her walk down the hall, open the closet door, and close it again. As her footsteps returned, Isabelle noticed that the rain was letting up. Then, a beam of sunshine peeked through a small opening in the clouds.

"Mother, you were right!" she exclaimed. "The storm is passing!"

Handing Isabelle her umbrella and raincoat, Tilda said, "We'd best be on our way. The rain will likely be gone by the time we reach the stadium."

Isabelle concluded that every resident of Centerport must have bought a ticket to the game by the way neighbors began emerging from their homes to form a flow of pedestrians headed toward the ball field. Although her mother had been right in predicting that the worst of the rain had passed, a mist remained in the air, changing occasionally to sprinkles throughout the first seven innings of the game.

As Isabelle rose to stretch her legs, she silently thanked the Lord that the start of the game had been delayed by

184

only a quarter of an hour, that the stands were nearly filled to capacity, and that Erskine was making a decent showing for itself, having put the only run on the board during the fifth inning, compliments of her brother. Taking her seat again, she watched with pride as he and Jack trotted to their field positions at the first two bases.

From second base, Jack could see Isabelle and her mother halfway up in the stands, slightly left of home plate. Their presence made him try all the harder, his senses growing especially keen when the first batsman in the eighth inning, a leftie, found King's slightly outside pitch and wholloped it into right field to get on base.

The next fellow up, a right hander, connected with an outside pitch, too.

Knox nabbed the ball and sent it to Jack.

Jack toed the bag and pegged it to Tracy.

Tracy tagged the runner and returned the ball to King.

Though this was only the second time the shortstop-to second-to first double play had been made in a game, it felt routine to Jack, thanks to the extra hours of practice.

King dispatched the first half of the eighth by following up with a strike-out, and Jack prayed that his upcoming turn at the plate would prove more fruitful than in past innings, but when he took the batter's box, the old problem of rhythm reared its head. He swung either too early or too late adding his name to the score sheet once more as a strike-out.

Unable to increase their lead in either this inning or the ninth, the score at the end of the contest stood unchanged from what it had been in the fifth inning, Erskine over Sutherland, 1-0. To the cheers of nearly two thousand fans,

185

Jack ran off the field to deposit his glove with his other belongings at the bench, well aware that his next performance, driving the Oldsmobile from its tarped position behind third base to the center of the infield, would be far more closely scrutinized than his play at second base.

While Hanson, Tracy, and the captain of the Sutherland team, megaphones in hand, carried the box of ticket stubs to the pitcher's mound, Jack hustled to the Oldsmobile where Mr. T was already beginning to untie the tarp. As the murmurs of excitement and anticipation rippled through the crowd, Jack worked rapidly to loosen the knot at the front end, maintaining perfect confidence that despite damp weather the automobile would spring to life without hesitation and chug admirably onto the wet field.

But when he lifted the tarp, he was shocked at what he saw. Rather than the distinctive toboggan front end, he discovered a wooden frame fashioned to imitate the shape of the automobile—which was missing!

Instantly, Jack dropped the tarp back in place. At the rear, astonishment and bewilderment deepened the lines of Mr. T's countenance.

A man in the stands called out, "Where's the Oldsmobile?"

Jack ignored him, motioning for Mr. T to join him as he headed toward Coach Hanson and the team captains.

More voices from the stands demanded to see the automobile.

Others began chanting, "We want the Olds!"

At the pitcher's mound, Hanson had grown impatient. "Get that Oldsmobile out here! The fans are waiting!"

Mr. T spoke first. "There ain't no Oldsmobile, coach."

Tracy's cheeks colored. "What are you talking about?"

Jack explained. "Someone took it from beneath the tarp and left a wooden frame in its place."

The Sutherland captain shook his head in puzzled disbelief.

Angrily, Hanson turned to him. "Did your fellows swipe the automobile as a prank? 'Cause if they did, I'll have the hide of each and every one of 'em!"

The Sutherland captain backed away. "I don't know anything about it! Honest!"

Sensing his sincerity, Jack was about to come to his defense when several fans streamed down onto the field.

Leading the indignant entourage was a corpulent fellow who ripped the tarp from the wooden frame, shouting, "See! There ain't no automobile! It's all a scam!"

Shouts of others followed.

"It's a swindle!"

"We've been cheated!"

The heavy-set ringleader broke off a portion of the frame. Wielding it like a bat, he and five like-sized cronies headed toward the pitcher's mound while dozens more fans hurried onto the field.

Panicked, Jack had begun looking for the best possible escape route when his gaze fell on a sight he never in his life expected to behold.

CHAPTER

18

Jack blinked, certain he must be imagining things. But when he opened his eyes again, the same remarkable scene came into focus. From the opening in the stands behind home plate emerged the 1901 Oldsmobile, Sheriff Brogan driving! He was followed by half a dozen deputies on horseback who formed flanks, three on either side.

As they started across the infield toward the pitcher's mound, cheers filled the stadium.

Mr. T pointed and grumbled. "Those horses are tearin' up my turf!"

Too relieved to care, Jack said, "I'll help you repair it."

By the time the law squad was halfway to the mound, the corpulent fan had lowered his stick and begun backing away.

Bringing the Oldsmobile to a halt beside the pitcher's mound, Sheriff Brogan stepped down and borrowed Coach Hanson's megaphone.

"Order in the stands! There'll be no drawing for this automobile 'till everyone is seated!"

The largest protester turned and headed toward his seat, directing others to do the same.

Burning with curiosity, Jack asked the sheriff, "Where did you find the Oldsmobile?"

"On River Road headed for the county line."

"But who—"

Brogan answered the question before Jack could complete it. "A fella name of Billings says he took it as a prank."

Tracy's expression darkened. "Billings!?"

Hanson said, "That figures."

Brogan explained further. "He claimed he planned to return it, but I could tell he was just concoctin' some tale to get himself off the hook." To Jack, he said, "I informed Mr. Billings that I was mighty familiar with this particular automobile and your team's plans to hold a drawing for it this afternoon. Then I tossed Billings in the clink and me and my deputies set out for Centerport."

Hanson said, "Much obliged, sheriff. You arrived in a nick of time."

A mischievous twinkle in his eyes, Brogan admitted, "I drove a little faster than I shoulda. My deputies were hard put to keep up—they were supposed to be out front as my escort!"

Sensing an opportunity, Jack said, "You could use an automobile to help keep order in the county. Sure you don't want to buy a ticket? It's not too late to enter the drawing."

Brogan shook his head. "I'll leave the winning to someone else." Seeing that the field had cleared of spectators, he said, "Speaking of which, it's about time you got on with that drawing, don't you think?"

Retrieving his megaphone from the sheriff, Coach Hanson addressed the fans. "And now, what you've all been waiting for. Captain Parnell of the Sutherland team will draw the winner of the 1901 Oldsmobile."

With great flare, Tracy knelt to remove the padlock

from the latch, opened the lid, and stirred up the contents.

Parnell turned his head away from the box, reached down inside, and scrambled the tickets some more before pulling one out.

A hush rippled through the audience.

Studying the ticket carefully, Parnell raised the megaphone to his mouth. "The winner of the 1901 Oldsmobile is . . . " he checked the ticket stub one more time . . . "Thaddeus Tuttle!"

Mr. T said under his breath, "Can't be."

Parnell repeated the name. "Thaddeus Tuttle. Are you here?"

Seeing that Mr. T was too overcome with shock to speak, Jack said, "He's right here!"

Coach Hanson raised his megaphone. "The winner of the Oldsmobile is Thaddeus Tuttle. Congratulations!"

Cheers and applause erupted, quickly drowning out the smattering of boos from a few disgruntled losers.

Mr. T remained rooted to his beloved turf as he stared at the automobile. "Can't be mine. I didn't enter the drawing."

Jack said, "Then someone must have entered for you. Come on, I'll show you how to run your new machine."

Mr. T sat behind the tiller, a curious mix of awe, happiness, and disbelief brightening the deep crevasses of his weathered complexion. Within minutes, the Oldsmobile made its way out of the stadium much as it had entered, flanked on either side by sheriff's deputies and cheered by almost two thousand spectators.

But late that night, as Jack lay in bed pondering Mr. T's happy surprise, and the financial and athletic victories of his team, he still had a feeling of emptiness inside. He knew what was missing, and that he would not find peace until he had taken certain steps down the path the Lord was laying before him. With a prayer for guidance and strength, he mentally mapped out the journey, determined to make a start on the morrow.

The next morning when Isabelle helped her mother serve breakfast, the Erskine nine and substitutes were full of talk of the previous day's victory, and laughing over Billings' foiled attempt to abscond with the Oldsmobile. But Isabelle couldn't help noticing that Jack barely smiled. Neither did he comment.

Puzzled over the cause for his seeming unhappiness, she planned to ask him about it when the meal had ended and her work in the kitchen was finished. But before she and her mother had put away the dishes, Jack appeared at the kitchen door, his somber expression unchanged.

"Mrs. Dorlon, Isabelle, may I please have a word with you when you're finished here?"

At Isabelle's nod, her mother said, "Give us a few more minutes, then meet us in the parlor."

When Jack had gone, Tilda asked Isabelle, "What's this all about?"

Isabelle shrugged. "I guess we'll just have to wait and see."

Minutes passed like hours as Isabelle stacked clean plates, cups, and saucers in the cupboards and tidied up the kitchen shelf. Helping her mother to sort and put away the last of the silverware, they hung up their aprons and headed toward the parlor.

Seemingly by chance, Tracy descended the stairs, reaching the hall outside the parlor door at the exact same time. "Going to speak with Jack, too, I assume?"

His mother asked, "What's on his mind, do you know?"

Tracy smiled enigmatically. "I'll leave it to Jack to explain."

Jack rose when the Dorlons entered. He tried—but didn't quite succeed—in offering a smile. Thinking of the words he was about to say, his heart began to race. Focusing on Tilda Dorlon as she settled into the chair by the door, his words came in fits and starts.

"I . . . wanted to . . . " He shifted his weight and began anew. "I have something important to ask you." His gaze taking in Tracy and Isabelle who occupied the couch, he added, " . . . all of you." Perching nervously on the edge of the chair nearest Isabelle's mother, he pleaded silently for God's grace, then looked into the woman's kind eyes. His gaze steady, words began to tumble out. "Mrs. Dorlon, I love your daughter. I want to marry her—not now, but a year from June, when I've graduated. I've already informed my folks of my plan, and they have no objections."

Jack's focus shifted to Isabelle. The look he gave her, so full of longing with more than a trifle of apprehension mixed in, dissolved her heart into a pool of pure love.

He continued. "I've discussed my feelings and my plans with Isabelle, too, of course, and she says she'll promise herself to me."

Isabelle wanted desperately to reply, *Yes, Jack! I promise myself to you!* but the words remained trapped behind the baseball-sized lump in her throat.

To Tracy, Jack said, "You've known for some time how I feel about your sister."

Tracy nodded. "I'd be pleased to have you as my brother-in-law."

Addressing Tilda Dorlon once again, Jack said, "So I'd like to ask your permission to marry Isabelle next June." Before she could respond, he quickly added, "I know it would be best to have her visit my home before we're engaged—see where I grew up and all—but I just—I just have to ask you now, or I'll never have any peace!"

Tilda smiled. "It appears to me, young man, that you've got your bases covered. Isabelle is willing to have you. Your folks agree to the match. Tracy wants you for a brother-in-law. And I'd be honored to have you as a son-in-law!"

Tracy grinned. "Sounds like you've hit a home run, Weatherby!"

Solemn still, Jack went to Isabelle and dropped to one knee, taking her hand in his. "Isabelle Dorlon," his voice barely exceeded a whisper, "will you marry me?"

Forcing words past the stubborn clot in her throat, she replied, "Yes! Of course I will!"

Getting to his feet, Tracy clapped Jack on the shoulder. "Congratulations, Weatherby! This is quite a victory for you! I hope the Erskine nine are equally successful when we play Robinson!"

Following her son out of the room, Tilda Dorlon said, "Welcome to the Dorlon family, Mr. Weatherby."

Jack was too elated over his engagement and too entranced by the sparkle lighting Isabelle's dark eyes to acknowledge the comments with more than a nod. Rising to his feet, he drew Isabelle from her chair. Hands cradling her pretty, oval face, he lowered his mouth to hers, tasting the sweet honey of her lips.

Isabelle closed her eyes, delighting in the tenderness of Jack's kiss, gentle as a bee extracting nectar from a delicate blossom. When the magic moment ended, he wrapped his arms about her, his closeness shrouding her in the security of his love.

Moments passed—she wasn't certain how many—when the voices and footsteps of her mother, Tracy, Anthony, and Gregory in the hallway caused them to part.

Only reluctantly did Jack release Isabelle, saying, "I guess it's time for church." The three-quarter-hour bells of the mantle clock and chimes from the steeple a few blocks distant confirmed his observation. Taking her hand firmly in his, they emerged from the parlor to receive the best wishes and congratulations bestowed by Anthony and Gregory.

As they walked the three blocks to church, Isabelle perceived the world—her sunny, splendid world—in a whole new way. Dew drops on lilac blossoms sparkled like diamonds, releasing their perfume to overspread the village, just as the tune of the carillon was sending forth its lilting melody for all to hear. If greater happiness were possible, she could only imagine it coming on her wedding day thirteen months from now, for today, *this day*, possessed a unique enchantment all its own.

Along the way, Jack tried to think how he could make this day memorable for Isabelle. He had no betrothal gift to give her, nor could he afford to purchase one even if the stores were open, which they never were on Sundays. Then they arrived at church to find Mr. T and his Oldsmobile at the curb surrounded by curious parishioners, and an idea came to him.

When services were over and the opportunity arose, he spoke privately with the old groundskeeper, then he reclaimed Isabelle from a circle of young ladies who were making a fuss over news of her betrothal.

Pressing her hand into the crook of his arm, he said, "I hope you haven't made any plans for this afternoon, because I'd like us to spend it together."

"What are we going to do?" she asked eagerly.

He grinned and winked. "I'll tell you later."

"But how will I know what to wear if I don't know—"

"The dress you have on right now is just fine," he informed her. Noticing for the first time the ruffle of pink silk encircling her high collar and the tiny tucks setting off her bodice, he added, "In fact, it's more than just fine. It's the prettiest thing I've ever seen."

Isabelle smiled. She wanted to tell him she'd been wearing the same dress to church every week for the past month, but instead she kept her counsel.

Two hours later, when dinner ended and she was helping her mother clear the table, she noticed that Jack and Tracy took off without a word. They returned as she was putting away the last of the dishes.

Jack came to the kitchen to fetch her. Taking her by the hand, he led her down the hall and out the front door, careful to leave Chips inside.

At the curb stood Mr. T's Oldsmobile. Tied crosswise atop the storage area at the back was a canoe, bottom up, its pointed ends extending so far beyond the vehicle's width as to appear comical.

She chuckled. "It looks like you've planned a canoe ride."

"I thought we could spend a quiet hour or two alone on the water." Leading her to the Oldsmobile, he paused to stare at the boat and laugh before helping her in. "I guess we *will* look pretty silly, driving down the street this way."

"It's only a mile to the lagoon," she reminded him, adding, "on a Sunday, few will be about on the streets to notice us."

But the lagoon could be a different story altogether, she knew. Especially in May. Many Centerporters, tired of cool and rainy April days, liked to take to the shore in spring sunshine and warmth such as this. She held no hopes that they would have the lagoon to themselves, but she wouldn't mind sharing it.

As Jack cranked up the motor machine and set it in motion toward the shore, she pondered the realization that he had come a long way on conquering his fear of water, and the thought pleased her greatly. That, coupled with their betrothal made her feel lighter than air, happier than a bluebird on high, and certain that nothing could diminish her happiness.

She began to wonder about his sense of direction, however, when he chugged right past the road to the lagoon.

"Jack! Stop! You missed the turn!" she informed him, pointing the way.

"No, I didn't," he replied, his course and speed unaltered.

"But—"

"I never said we were going to the lagoon."

"Where, then?"

He grinned. "Be patient. You'll see."

CHAPTER

19

Jack drove along the harbor, heading out of town on a road that followed closely the shoreline of the big lake. Isabelle prayed he wasn't planning to launch the canoe in that great body of water, for calm as it appeared at the moment, she knew from experience that a storm could blow in quickly and they could be swamped and sunk before making it to shore.

Her apprehensions vanished when he turned down a country road leading inland. Over hill and dale he drove, covering mile after mile of rolling farm country with spring fields ready for plowing, sunny green pastures dotted with dairy cows, and pretty white farm houses aside huge red barns. When an hour had passed, she wondered how much farther they would have to go to reach their destination. She was about to ask when Jack turned down a shady lane whose entrance was marked by bent pussy willow branches. They slowly made their way along the hilly, curving driveway until a yellow brick mansion overlooking a hidden lake came into view.

"Who lives here?" Isabelle asked with wonder.

"No one but Charlie, the caretaker, right now," Jack replied. "But during the summer, the place is occupied by some Chicago folks Mr. T worked for thirty-three years ago. He rang up Charlie to ask if we could come out here for the afternoon."

Passing a gazebo rich with fancy, delicate decorations, Jack brought the Oldsmobile to a halt beside the only dock on the placid lake. Gazing across the mirror surface, he silently thanked the Lord for the beauty of this place, reflecting its perimeter of budding trees bursting forth with new life. He thanked God, too, for the promise Isabelle had made to him this day, and for His help in conquering his fear of water sufficiently to mark the occasion with a canoe ride.

No sooner had he set about untying the canoe than a fellow of about fifty clad in grass-stained overalls came along.

"You must be Mr. Weatherby," he said with a smile.

Jack nodded. "And you must be Charlie."

The hired man nodded in turn. Running his hand over the toboggan curve of the front end, he said, "So this here's the Oldsmobile Thaddeus won on account of you. Ain't she somethin'?" He admired the machine a moment longer, then helped with the task of removing the canoe from the back and launching it from a sandy patch of shoreline beside the dock.

Handing the bow line to Jack, he said, "You and your miss have yourselves a pleasant afternoon. I'll fuel up the Olds so she's ready for your drive home."

"Much obliged," Jack replied, holding the boat steady while Isabelle stepped in.

She settled on the bow seat and unfolded a parasol adorned in row upon row of pale pink lace the exact shade of her dress. On her right wrist fluttered the bow of baby blue satin ribbon she had tied there. And on her face was the affectionate look of a young lady mirroring back to him the admiration, love, and happiness he was feeling in his own heart. Conversation seemed unnecessary as he paddled to the opposite side of the small basin then toured the circumference, but eventually words came forth as he pondered the privacy and beauty of the lake, the majesty of the square mansion overlooking it, and the charm of the matching yellow gazebo near the water's edge.

"I can't help wondering if the people who own this place ever enjoy it half as much as I am right now."

"It is lovely," Isabelle agreed, adding thoughtfully, "but if I owned it, I'd give it all up for the ability to read."

Jack pondered her statement, replying, "And if *I* owned it, I'd give it all up for a victory over Robinson next month."

Isabelle laughed. "I guess neither one of us puts much store in worldly riches."

"It's probably just as well," he allowed, feeling so blessed with the promise of her love and the gift of God's grace that he was certain all the money on earth could not purchase an hour of happiness equal to this.

Five weeks later, memories of the canoe ride on the hidden lake had faded little in Isabelle's mind as she rode the rails to River Bend for the much-anticipated match with Robinson College. Again, she was invited to ride and dine with Judith Jamison in her father's private railroad car, and to lodge with the Shandlers upon arrival.

Anthony was along, too. Not only would he take responsibility for a business transaction for Jamison Hardware in River Bend, but he and Judith, now engaged, had set their wedding date in October, and a discussion regarding pertinent details dominated the conversation as the train clacked toward its destination.

Arrival in the distant city entailed none of the problems of their previous visit, the Shandlers' Cadillac having been fitted out with four brand new tires. Entering the stadium, they met up with Judge Whittaker, taking their place with four hundred or so other Erskine supporters. Isabelle well remembered her previous visit two months ago when Jack spared her the ignominy of being beaned in the head with a foul ball. She prayed the calamity wouldn't repeat itself today. With the judge by her side to throw up his thick arm for protection if necessary, she probably had nothing to worry about.

As she gazed out upon the field, she saw that it was now well-groomed, though not to the perfection of Mr. T's field. The hardwoods beyond had unfurled their foliage now, their greenery complimenting that of the turf and obscuring the roof lines in the quadrangles which were formerly visible.

Seeing the thousands of Robinson fans filling in the stands around her, she said a prayer of thanks for the blessings that had allowed the Erskine nine to be here today. Across the diamond, the band leader struck up the Robinson band in a lusty rendition of their school song, rousing cheers from the supporters of their brown stockings which incited an immediate response from the vocal supporters of the purple. Waving her Erskine pennant, Isabelle chimed in with those around her, singing their pep song to the tune of *John Brown's Body.*

Purple is the color of the stalwart and the brave;
Purple are the banners that the conq'ring heroes wave
Purple are the violets above the lonely grave

200

Of poor old Robinson!
>Glory, glory to the Purple!
>Glory, glory to the Purple!
>Glory, glory to the Purple!
And down with Robinson!

From the moment the ball was thrown out to start the game, until the beginning of the sixth inning, Isabelle remained on the edge of her seat. Robinson had placed players on bases in every inning except the second. When in the field, their pitcher had given up no hits. Erskine was being outplayed, and the fact that Robinson did not now lead by several tallies was due only to the inability to make hits at the right time.

It was anybody's game. Stiles went to bat. On the Erskine stand the cheering died away and the purple flags ceased waving and fluttering in the still afternoon air. Across the diamond the band laid aside its instruments and the shadow of the western stand crept along the turf until its edge touched the line of white that marked the coacher's box. On the Erskine bench, Jack leaned forward anxiously.

Focusing on Stiles once more, Isabelle watched him thrust his cap back and grip his bat determinedly. Vose, the pitcher, let the ball fly. Stiles hit a short grounder. The first baseman scooped it up and tagged the bag before Stiles was halfway there.

Tracy went to bat next. Two strikes were called. He connected with the next pitch, sending a high foul into the hands of the left fielder. With a look of disgust, he tossed aside his bat and paused on his way back to the bench to whisper into Jack's ear before he stepped into the batter's box. Whatever the advice, it didn't stop Jack from falling victim to the deceptive curves of the merciless Vose. Head down, expression woeful, Isabelle's heart went with Jack as he drew on his glove and headed to his position at second base.

The Robinson band struck up again, and the Erskine contingent, determined to re-affirm their loyalty, started cheering once more while the purple-sleeved players spread out over the diamond.

The umpire, a rotund little man in a navy blue blouse shirt, ran nimbly to his position while Stiles thumped his big mitten and King picked up the ball. The first batsman was the Robinson captain, a center fielder named Wood. Three slow balls were all King needed for a strike-out. The next batsman, Brown, performed no better, and Isabelle joyfully added her flag and voice to the waving and cheering of those around her.

When Regan, the Robinson right fielder stepped to the plate, Isabelle was certain the inning was over. From her previous trip to River Bend, she remembered him as a poor batsman. King sent a straight, slow ball to the outside corner drawing a strike, then repeated the routine. She waited for him to do the same a third time, but instead, the ball floated over the center of the plate.

Regan sent it arching toward third and raced for the bag. Erskine's man let it slip through his fingers. By the time it had been recovered, the runner was safe.

Isabelle saw Hanson send Erskine's backup pitcher, Dunham, to the bull pen as Vose took up his bat. Even with a tired arm, Isabelle had confidence that King could retire his opponent. Whether from sheer doggedness or a sudden stroke of divine grace, Vose found the second pitch that came his way and hit it safely into right field. Regan took second. Then Cox, the head of the batting list, stepped up to the plate and swung his ash wickedly while he waited.

The umpire called one strike, then another, then two balls. Cox swung again. With the crack of his bat, he sent the ball out past shortstop. Regan reached third. With two outs, the bases were full.

Hanson called Dunham in from the bull pen and held a conference with him and Stiles at the mound. Up next was the Brown's catcher, one of their best batters. He tapped the plate as though he were sure to bring in a run.

Dunham's first pitch went wide and Stiles's brilliant stop brought forth a burst of applause. Two strikes followed.

Then the batsman crossed the plate, suddenly becoming a left-hander. Dunham couldn't seem to adjust, his next two pitches going outside. He dug his toe into the mound, considering his dilemma, then wound up and let fly.

The umpire made his pronouncement.

"Ball three!"

Dunham straightened his arms, swung his foot, and hurled the ball waist high for the plate. The batsman connected, but not squarely. The ball soared. The men on bases raced for home.

The sphere descended toward third, but Erskine's baseman muffed!

Regan scored.

Vose passed third. The baseman recovered the ball and threw it straight to the plate. Vose slid. Stiles's right hand swept down and tagged him.

The umpire judged with confidence.

"Out!"

Isabelle watched with dread as Regan's run went up on

the scoreboard—Robinson-1. With the big goose egg still showing for the Erskine side, she prayed for fewer errors and better hitting in the seventh inning. But the players swapped sides twice with no change in score, despite the fact that Erskine had managed to do some hitting against the previously indefatigable Vose.

The top of the eighth saw Stiles again in the batter's box. But unlike his last time up, he made a clean hit to the outfield just over shortstop's head. Isabelle, Judge Whittaker, and their fellow supporters burst into wild cheers.

Tracy selected his bat and went to the plate. Vose settled the ball in his hands, tapped the dust with his brass-toed shoe, and glanced sharply toward Stiles. When he turned quickly to pitch, the ball went wide striking Tracy on the hip. With the wave of the umpire's hand, he went limping to first and Stiles jogged to second. A rhythmic *Erskine! Erskine! Erskine!* rang out from the stands.

With a silent prayer and words of instruction from Coach Hanson, Jack adjusted his cap, wiped his perspiring hands on his trousers, and gripped his bat. Vose eyed him intently. Jack smiled despite his nervousness.

The muscles in the back of his legs were twitching as he took a couple of swings to loosen up, then stepped into the box. The first pitch headed inside. Jack swung anyway—intentionally late. Now that he'd given a false reading to the pitcher, he waited patiently.

Two balls came across. Then a strike. Then Jack saw what he wanted. Turning a trifle to his left, he brought the stick around easily. A bunt rolled neatly inside the third base line.

By the time Jack reached first, Stiles was safe at third and Tracy was sliding for second.

In the Erskine stand, Isabelle was on her feet, pennant waving, as she and the Judge ripped into another verse of the pep song, joined by several others.

Robinson is wavering, her pride's about to fall;
Robinson is wavering, she cannot hit the ball;
Erskine is the winner, for her team's the best of all;
Oh, poor old Robinson!

Bissell went to bat. Vose, calm of face, surveyed the bases while his supporters shouted words of encouragement. Jack prepared to run. Before the pitcher's arm was well back, he started like an express train toward second. Simultaneously, Stiles made as though to dash home and Tracy played off half-way to third.

Vose delivered a wild pitch. His catcher struggled, caught it, and threw to second in error.

Stiles slid across the plate before the ball reached the second baseman. Jack flew back toward first, pausing halfway. Tracy, caught on his way to third, danced back and forth, the ball crossing time and again over his head.

Then he stumbled. The shortstop was on him in a flash. He crawled to his feet, dusted the loam from his shirt, and trotted off the field while Jack slid for second, beating the ball.

With the score tied, a man on second, and only one out, the Erskine stand went wild, flags and caps flying in the air. When they had calmed down, Bissell stepped into the batter's box once again. With a crack of his bat, he sent the ball arching high toward right field. The fielder did his job admirably. The ball sped quickly home, but not soon enough to keep Jack from reaching third.

The Robinson band went bravely to work once more, brass and bass drum pouring forth in solid support. Not to be outdone, Isabelle joined the judge, leading a unison cheer from supporters of the purple.

Erskine! Erskine! Erskine! Rah! Rah! Rah!

Knox came to bat. The stands settled down. Isabelle saw messages passing from Tracy to Knox, then to Jack who nodded. She watched intently as Vose faced Knox with self-assurance. In fact, the opponents were so confident, their outfield came in a bit.

The count was soon three balls, one strike. The fourth pitch was a drop. Knox struck at it hard, dropped his bat, and flew toward first. The catcher stopped the ball on the ground, stood up, glared in confusion at first, then threw it there, evidently thinking it had been the third strike.

Meanwhile, Jack headed warily toward home. The first baseman hurled the ball back, too late for the catcher to tag him out. The run put the purple ahead, prompting pandemonium in the Erskine stand.

Knox trotted back to the plate and picked up his bat while Jack headed for the bench, dusty, panting, and pleased to accept the slaps and pats of his teammates. Robinson's coach argued to return him to third but Tracy's strategy prevailed and Vose went back to work. A moment later, Knox was walking to first, and seconds after that, he had stolen second. Lowe bunted toward first and beat the ball to the base. Knox took third.

A wild pitch allowed Lowe to advance to second. Knox made no attempt to score. Then Northup came to bat.

He bided his time. Two strikes were called. He found the next ball fairly and drove a grounder into right field.

Knox jogged home. Lowe streaked to third. Northup sat down on first to tie his shoe.

Dunham went to bat. He swung at a drop that hit the plate. Northup attempted to steal second. When he was tagged four feet from the bag, the top half of the eighth inning came to an end.

Isabelle gazed with pleasure at the scoreboard: Erskine-3; Robinson-1. Watching Jack hustle to his position at second base, she couldn't help feeling proud of the man to whom she had promised herself—strong, hard-working, devoted. Now, if he and his team could prevent Robinson from scoring, his long-held dream would come true.

The Erskine nine took a significant step closer to their goal when Dunham dismissed Robinson's first three batters in a series of strike-outs. Cheering broke forth anew, loud and triumphant, as the teams changed sides and Motter came to bat.

But hopes of increasing the lead of the purple diminished when he struck out and Stiles was thrown out at first. Then Tracy hit a line drive into right field, gaining first base. Isabelle prayed Jack would be equally successful, but he flied out miserably to Vose.

Some of the supporters left their seats to crowd along the base lines as the teams changed sides, but Isabelle and the judge remained in the stands on their feet. Dunham picked up the ball. Stiles donned his mask. Tracy thumped his mitt. Jack, at second, shifted from one foot to the other, and even at a distance, Isabelle could sense his joy.

The Robinson batsman, their catcher, stepped to the plate. Isabelle assumed he would be an easy victim until Dunham struck him on the elbow. Cheers from his supporters thundered over the field as he took first.

The next batter had already proven his mettle as a hard hitter. When he connected with the second pitch, Isabelle took solace in the fact that it was a catchable fly ball to center field. But Bissell couldn't seem to find it in the glare of late afternoon sun. When the play ended, runners stood on first and third.

Robinson's next batsman hit a slow grounder toward Dunham. Pausing to make sure that the man on third wouldn't try to score, he threw to first too late. The bases were full!

Brown banners flaunted and gyrated in the air, casting strange dancing silhouettes against the turf. The shadow of the western stand had lengthened across the infield. Behind it, the sky was aglow with orange, while toward the village a golden haze filled the air.

Tension grew. Spectators shouted instructions to their favorite players. Robinson's band lit into a rapid, rousing rendition of their school song.

The Erskine response, split by the distance between those at the baseline and those still in the stands, echoed faintly. The next batsman stepped to the plate, chin thrust forward. Stiles squatted behind him.

At second, beads of perspiration formed on Jack's forehead. Silently, he prayed that the remainder of the inning would be played with good judgment, error-free. His gaze roved to Tracy at first, carelessly flipping a pebble across the grass, then to Northup in right field, motionless with his hand shading his eyes. Dunham drew his hand across his forehead in an idle fashion. Then his arms shot up and he delivered the first pitch.

The batsman let it pass.

Confidently, the umpire called a strike.

The Erskine contingent applauded, then fell silent when the umpire called balls on the next two pitches.

Coaches shouted directions. Runners crouched down, ready to sprint. Dunham delivered the next pitch.

The batsman swung and missed. Again, the supporters of the Purple shouted and waved their pennants.

Dunham glanced around the bases, settled himself, and let loose with the next pitch.

Ball met bat.

The sphere arced toward second. Jack squinted into the sinking sun. The ball was on a path high above his head. He took two steps back, sprang straight up, and pulled the ball in.

Isabelle was certain Jack had put at least two feet of air between himself and the turf before making the catch. Coaches shouted for runners to return to their bases.

Jack took two broad steps to second base, then threw to Motter at third. The runner caught between third and home doubled back. Arms outstretched, he launched himself toward the bag.

The umpire swung his hand in a circle toward the bases, calling with finality, "Game!"

Isabelle waved her pennant frantically, her fading voice drowned out by the exuberant cheers of fellow supporters. Those at the baseline flooded onto the field in a wave, lifting players to their shoulders. Her heart overflowed with pride and thankfulness, seeing Jack carried off the field in triumphant glory!

But as she made her way out through the stadium gate with Judith and Anthony, the sight that caught her eye changed her smile to a scowl and caused her to turn her head aside.

Anthony immediately sensed her uneasiness. "What's the matter, Isabelle? You look as if you've seen a ghost!"

"I wish it *were* a ghost. Look behind me."

Anthony grumbled. "Reginald Billings. And he's giving you a good looking-over."

Chills ran down Isabelle's spine despite the warmth of the June day.

Judith asked, "Was he the one who made off with the 1901 Oldsmobile just before the drawing?"

Isabelle nodded, explaining briefly the other troublesome encounters.

Anthony said, "I'm surprised to see him here. I thought he was still in the Lakeshore County jail."

Isabelle replied, "So did I. Evidently, he's paid for his crime and now he's a free man again."

Judith told Isabelle, "No matter. Just forget about that rascal and think about tonight. We're sure to enjoy the operetta by the Robinson College Players. And the dinner afterward at the Riverside Terrace will be nothing short of splendid."

Anthony added, "And Billings won't be anywhere in sight."

Isabelle forced a smile. "You're right."

But despite her friends' assurances, she couldn't seem to erase Billings' image from her mind.

CHAPTER

20

At the operetta held in the Robinson College auditorium—the same place where Anthony had obtained victory in his debate concerning the automobile—Isabelle laughed so hard her sides ached. The Music Department in conjunction with the English Department had written and scored an original comedy inspired by the rivalries of the debate and baseball teams. Arguments over the automobile ran from the ignorant to the absurd. The plot even included a drawing for an automobile to raise money for the Robinson nine. A fictitious Centerport lawyer and former Robinson player put up his vehicle for the drawing, only to have it stolen by an ousted team member who couldn't keep it running long enough to drive out of River Bend. In a plot twist that defied reality, the would-be villain—a mechanical genius of sorts—suffered a change of heart while repairing the cantankerous motor machine, returning a much-improved version to center field in time for the drawing.

Cheers, whistles, and applause that seemed never-ending brought cast and crew on stage for bows and encores three times before the audience had had their fill. Afterward, Jack escorted Isabelle to one of the streetcars in front of the college which had been reserved to transport the team members and their friends to the Riverside Ter-

211

race.

The terrace level of the restaurant had been appropriately decorated with pennants, caps, and shirts from both teams, as well as bats, balls, gloves, and even a couple of salt bags. A sign congratulating Erskine on their victory, and another wishing Robinson better luck next year, hung prominently on opposing walls. The tables for four had been set with place cards matching Robinson players with Erskine players of like positions. With Jack's help, Isabelle was soon seated by the window at the table designated for second basemen and their girls.

Favors included a live purple orchid for Isabelle— Erskine's color—and a white one with brown speckles for the Robinson girl who had not yet arrived. As Isabelle took in her surroundings, she discovered that the most intriguing aspect of the terrace room was its opening onto a lighted riverside garden.

Gazing out the window at the gaslit blossoms and tile walkways, she said to Jack, "Promise me we'll take a walk outside after dinner. The lilies are too lovely to ignore."

He grinned. "That's an easy enough promise to keep." Picking up her orchid, he tucked it above her ear. "Until then, you'll have to content yourself with this."

She left it in her hair for a moment, then removed it to study it, explaining, "I believe I'd rather have it on the table, where I can appreciate it."

She set it aside moments later, at the arrival of the Robinson second baseman, Cal Richman, and his girl, Mary Beth. Outgoing and ready to share amusing riddles and humorous anecdote, they helped the three course dinner of Erskine aspic, Robinson potatoes and steak, and home run sundaes to pass quickly, seasoned liberally with laughter as it was.

When their table partners excused themselves to visit with others, Jack told Isabelle, "I'd best keep my promise now, before too many others decide to visit the gardens and spoil their serenity."

Placing her hand on his arm, he escorted her out the glass door and along the walkway which was bordered by granite benches and cultivated oval plots planted with honeysuckle bushes. They were strolling toward the river's edge where dimmer lights revealed a dock and rowboats when Isabelle remembered the orchid she had left on the table.

"Jack, would you please go back and fetch my orchid?"

Pulling her close, he said, "For a kiss."

He began lowering his mouth to hers but she turned away. "Fetch my orchid before someone else takes it, then you'll get your kiss," she promised.

"All right," he grumbled. Settling for a peck on her cheek, he made hurried strides toward the terrace room.

Seeing a bench beyond the next bush, Isabelle had started toward it when someone grabbed her from behind, clamping a hand firmly over her mouth while his arm held her in a rib-crushing grip.

"I saw you spurn Weatherby's kiss, and well you should, the coward!"

Isabelle recognized Reginald Billings' voice instantly. With a violent twist, she dug her elbows into his stomach and tried to scream, but only a faint, muffled sound came out.

His hold tightened. Nearly lifting her off her feet, he dragged her behind the bush.

"Now, I'll show you what a *real* kiss is like!" he

threatened.

She fought the hand that tried to turn her toward him, simultaneously kicking her heel into his ankle.

"Ouch! You . . . "

"Let me go!" she cried, her hem ripping in the struggle.

Footsteps sounded on the walkway.

Billings' hand again closed off her mouth.

"Isabelle?"

It was Jack.

Struggling with all her might, she emitted a muffled cry for help.

In an instant, Jack was there, parting Billings from her. "You no good . . . " He pulled back to land a punch.

"Jack, don't!" Isabelle pleaded.

Too angry for self-control, Jack buried his fist in Billings' jaw, sending him to the ground.

Tracy seemed to appear out of nowhere. "Billings, what are you doing here?"

Jack replied for him. "Trying to steal a kiss from your sister, that's what!"

Tracy lunged instantly for Billings.

Isabelle grabbed him by the elbow. "Tracy, no! Fighting won't solve anything!"

Tracy pulled away. "You're in for it, now!" he warned Billings, picking him up by the collar.

Other teammates gathered.

Forcing Billings to face them, Tracy announced, "This no-good . . . tried to force a kiss on my sister! What are we going to do about it?"

Stiles said, "Throw him in the river! That'll cool him off!"

Others echoed the suggestion.

Moving en mass to accomplish the task, the nine picked Billings up and hauled him to the dock.

With Jack on one end and Tracy on the other, they swung him over the river to a unison count.

"One . . . two . . . three . . . "

Cheers erupted as Billings splashed down. Seeing him wade along the shore in a downriver direction, they congratulated one another and headed back toward the terrace room.

By Isabelle's side once more, Jack inspected the tear in her gown. "Are you all right?"

Laying her head against his broad chest, she snuggled close. "I am now."

Pulling her tight into his embrace, Jack prepared to kiss her, stopping midway to her mouth. "Uh, oh. I lost your orchid."

Pressing her lips against his, Isabelle allowed her kiss to deliver the thankfulness and love she was feeling in her heart. When it ended, she whispered, "That's all right. You can always get me another orchid."

As the train carrying the Erskine nine and their guests rolled into Centerport at half past noon the following day, Isabelle was astounded to discover from the window of Mr. Jamison's private railroad car that a massive crowd awaited them at the depot. She wondered if the college campus was at this moment abandoned, seeing what appeared to be the entire student body lining the platform, tracks, and streets as far as the eye could see. Congratulatory messages plastered across banners and signs rose in splendid salute, some specifically singling out Jack, who was seated in the car reserved for his team. She thought how pleased he must feel, being recognized for his hard work and the results it had brought.

Parked alongside the drive approaching the depot was the Jamisons' hired man in the Cadillac. Behind him were Mr. T in his Olds and three hired hacks waiting to haul the team and their coach in a victorious procession to the college.

Sizing up the mass of humanity between their railroad car and the Cadillac, Anthony told Judith and Isabelle, "Hold tight when we step onto the platform. I don't want either of you getting lost in this crowd."

Somehow, he found a way to squeeze between the members of the noisy, cheering, pennant-waving assembly, settling Judith and Isabelle in the Cadillac in time to watch the Erskine nine and Coach Hanson alight from their car to be borne atop the shoulders of friends and well-wishers to their vehicles. Coach Hanson was given a place of honor beside Mr. T, while Jack, Tracy, Stiles, and King occupied the first hack.

As the Cadillac proceeded slowly down the street, Isabelle's thoughts strayed from the pandemonium surrounding her. In three days, the term would come to an end. Tracy would graduate, then Jack would take her to his family's farm for a visit. After a week's stay, she would return home and Jack would move to River Bend for the balance of the summer where he would work as an aid to Judge Whittaker while playing on the newly formed River Bend Pirates amateur baseball team. She wondered how she could stand the separation from mid-June to early September. Already, she missed him!

Her deliberations were penetrated by loud neighing. Looking back, she could see that the horses of the third hack had become agitated and difficult.

From his seat in the first hack, Jack was aware of the horses' complaints, and the exact instant when student cries of congratulations turned troubled. The assemblage in front of his carriage struggled to crowd onto the sidewalk. The pounding of hooves sounded against the brick pavement, vibrating through the seat and up his spine. He turned to look.

Sweeping down the street swayed the third hack, its team plunging forward with outstretched heads. On the box, the driver tugged vainly at the lines and shouted warnings to the crowd.

Panic swept over Jack. Two hacks and two automobiles lay in its path. His own hack sprang forward. He prayed his driver's team and the one following them wouldn't run blind, too. Then four words pierced his heart.

Isabelle could be killed!

Instantly, he threw open the door and jumped out.

Barely maintaining his balance, he positioned himself to catch hold of the reins of the team bearing down upon him. Then, he leaped forward. Grabbing rein and mane, he clutched tightly, pressing all his weight back of the bit.

The horse's hooves grazed his legs at every plunge. He clung desperately, their speed undiminished. Seconds later, the horse's head came down. Jack's feet touched brick. Galloping strides slowed to a trot. Cries and cheers filled his ears.

In response, the horses veered violently, colliding into Reilly's General Merchandise. The blow of his back against the clapboard drove the air from Jack's lungs. He fell into darkness.

Isabelle scrambled from the tonneau seat of the Jamisons' Cadillac, lifted her skirt, and ran toward Jack. Pushing through the circle of strangers, she knelt beside his still, battered form and cradled his head in her lap.

"Lord, please don't let him die!" she quietly pleaded. Then, patting his face with her gloved hand, she ordered, "Jack! Wake up!"

He didn't stir.

Someone in the crowd hollered, "Go get Doc White!" The order echoed down the street.

A minute later, the physician knelt beside her, pulled a bottle of smelling salts from his bag, and held it beneath Jack's nose.

He shook his head and blinked, trying to focus on the face peering down at him.

"Isabelle?"

His voice was so faint, she could hardly hear him.

"Jack, are you all right?" she asked, her own voice a weak tremor.

He tried to make sense of his circumstances, then he remembered the runaway horses. "The hack . . . those horses . . . "

Isabelle touched her hand to his cheek. "You stopped them. No one got hurt but you."

Gradually regaining his orientation, he started to sit up.

Dr. White laid a hand on his shoulder. "Easy now, young man."

Tracy, his cheeks ruddy with concern, came and knelt next to his sister. "That was some ride you took, Weatherby."

218

Rising gradually to a sitting position, Jack rubbed the back of his head, a smile curving his mouth. "It was at that."

Stiles pressed through the thick circle of onlookers to gaze down at his injured teammate. "You must be trying to set a new standard for heroism on the nine. First, in the game yesterday, and now this. You're making the rest of us look bad!" He grinned.

Jack started to gain to his feet.

Isabelle clutched his elbow. "Jack, please!"

Dr. White said, "You'd better come to my office and let me check—"

Jack interrupted. "I'm fine Isabelle, Doc. Honest." As he straightened to brush the dirt and wrinkles from his pants, Coach Hanson and the rest of the Erskine nine crowded in. Lifting Jack to their shoulders, they bore him off toward Mr. T's Olds.

Isabelle sighed with relief, blinking away a happy tear. She had loved Jack for some time now, but this near trage-dy was revealing a new depth of devotion. As she watched him bobbing triumphantly above the crowd, she thanked the Lord that her betrothal had not ended prematurely on the sidewalk beside Reilly's General Merchandise, and that her beloved was once again on his way to the victory cele-bration he had dreamed of for so many years.

A year and three weeks later, as Isabelle waited in a small room off the narthex for her wedding ceremony to begin, she reflected briefly on that day outside Reilly's General Merchandise when she had nearly lost Jack. Again, she thanked God that the crisis had passed without lasting effects, and that this year's Erskine nine had completed their season with only two losses. But most of all, she thanked God that her special day had finally arrived, and that Judith—Mrs. Anthony Tidball—was serving as her matron of honor.

Judith had left her momentarily to check with her husband, who was serving as head usher, on progress in seating the guests. She returned now, face flushed, a folded paper in her trembling hand.

"I saw Jack."

"Is he nervous?" Isabelle wanted to know, since he'd suffered a slight case of stomach upset the previous day. Although he had denied it, she had attributed his queasiness to apprehension over their impending nuptials.

"He's about as shaky as I am. You should have seen him when he tried to give me this note. He was all thumbs, fumbling through his pockets. I hope he doesn't drop your ring."

The last thing Isabelle needed at this moment was one more reason to worry over Jack's nerves. As she fidgeted with the blue satin ribbon Mrs. Weatherby had tied around her right wrist, she noticed that her own hands were none too steady. She prayed for a sense of calmness to descend on everyone in the wedding party.

The prayer seemed to work. Her own hands were no longer trembling, and Judith appeared calmer as she opened the paper. "Jack gave me strict instructions that I'm to read this to you right now."

As she cleared her throat, Isabelle wished ardently that she had overcome her word blindness and could read Jack's message herself. But the Lord had not seen fit to lift that burden from her as yet, so she simply thanked Him for sending her a man to whom her inability to read was of no consequence.

Quietly, Judith began to read Jack's words.

"Isabelle, this is your inning, your day on the baseball diamond of holy matrimony, and no finer a contender has ever entered the ball park. Now, in these final moments before you take the field, I want to tell you how very much you have come to mean to me over these past eighteen months.

"I am so proud of you and all that you have accomplished despite your special challenge. I wish your father could be here with us to walk you down the aisle. I know he would have been as proud of you as I am.

"I know, too, that Tracy is a worthy substitute, and that your father will be here in spirit when your brother gives your hand to me. I cherish Tracy like a brother, and consider it a privilege to make him my brother-in-law.

"Your mother, my 'mother away from home,' is a very special lady. I thank God that she took me in as a roomer, and is ready to take me on as a son.

"But most of all, I thank God for you, my precious Isabelle. You're a home-run hitter in my book. You're batting a thousand, and your fielding is free of errors. In every possible way, you're at the top of your game!

"And now, as you round third and head down the home stretch, remember that you'll soon be safe in the arms of the one who loves you more than words, or any baseball metaphor can say. I'm over the fence, out of the park, crazy in love with you, Isabelle. And I know beyond a shadow of a doubt that a long, winning season awaits us!

"With all my love, your about-to-be husband, Jack.

"P.S. I never did ask how many children you want. Cousin Catherine says nine sounds like the right number

221

for us. What do you think?"

Isabelle smiled. As the wedding march began to play, she dabbed away the tear that threatened to trickle down her cheek.

Stepping into the narthex, she took her place by Tracy's side and prepared to join the captain of her team for a ball game that would surely last a lifetime.

More *Great Lakes Romances*

For prices and availability, contact:

Bigwater Publishing, P.O. Box 177, Caledonia, MI 49316

Mackinac

by

Donna Winters

First in the series of *Great Lakes Romances*

(Set at Grand Hotel, Mackinac Island, 1895)

Her name bespeaks the age in which she lives...but **Victoria Whitmore** is no shy, retiring Victorian miss. She finds herself aboard the *Algomah*, traveling from staid Grand Rapids to Michigan's fashionable Mackinac Island resort. Her journey is not one of pleasure; a restful holiday does not await her. Mackinac's Grand Hotel owes the Whitmores money—enough to save the furniture manufactory from certain financial ruin. It becomes Victoria's mission to venture to the island to collect the payment. At Mackinac, however, her task is anything but easy, and she finds more than she bargained for.

Rand Bartlett, the hotel manager, is part of that bargain. Accustomed to challenges and bent on making the struggling Grand a success, he has not counted on the challenge of Victoria—and he certainly has not counted on losing his heart to her.

The Captain and the Widow
by
Donna Winters
Second in the series of *Great Lakes Romances*
(Set in Chicago, South Haven, and
Mackinac Island, 1897)
Lily Atwood Haynes is beautiful, intelligent, and ahead of her time . . . but even her grit and determination have not prepared her for the cruel event on Lake Michigan that leaves her widowed at age twenty. It is the lake—with its fathomless depths and unpredictable forces—that has provided her livelihood. Now it is the lake that challenges her newfound happiness.

When **Captain Hoyt Curtiss**, her husband's best friend, steps in to offer assistance in navigating the choppy waters of Lily's widowhood, she can only guess at the dark secret that shrouds his past and chokes his speech. What kind of miracle will it take to forge a new beginning for *The Captain and the Widow? Note:* The Captain and the Widow *is a spin-off from* Mackinac.

Sweethearts of Sleeping Bear Bay
by
Donna Winters
Third in the series of *Great Lakes Romances*
(Set in the Sleeping Bear Dune region of
northern Michigan, 1898)

Mary Ellen Jenkins is a woman of rare courage and experience . . . One of only four females licensed as navigators and steamboat masters on the Western Rivers, she is accustomed to finding her way through dense fog on the Mississippi. But when she travels North for the first time in her twenty-nine years, she discovers herself unprepared for the havoc caused by a vaporous shroud off Sleeping Bear Point. And navigating the misty shoals of her own uncertain future poses an even greater threat to her peace of mind.

Self-confident, skilled, and devoted to his duties as Second Mate aboard the Lake Michigan sidewheeler, *Lily Belle,* **Thad Grant** regrets his promise to play escort to the petticoat navigator the instant he lays eyes on her plain face. Then his career runs aground. Can he trust this woman to guide him to safe harbor, or will the Lady Reb ever be able to overcome the great gulf between them? *Note:* Sweethearts of Sleeping Bear Bay *is a spin-off from* The Captain and the Widow.

Charlotte of South Manitou Island
by
Donna Winters
Fourth in the series of *Great Lakes Romances*
(Set on South Manitou Island,
Michigan, 1891-1898)

Charlotte Richards' carefree world turns upside down on her eleventh birthday . . . the day her beloved papa dies in a spring storm on Lake Michigan. Without the persistence of fifteen-year-old **Seth Trevelyn**, son of South Manitou Island's lightkeeper, she might never have smiled again. He shows her that life goes on, and so does true friendship.

When Charlotte's teacher invites her to the World's Columbian Exposition of 1893, Seth signs as crewman on the *Martha G.*, carrying them to Chicago. Together, Seth and Charlotte sail the waters of the Great Lake to the very portal of the Fair, and an adventure they will never forget. While there, Seth saves Charlotte from a near fatal accident. Now, seventeen and a man, he realizes his friendship has become something more. Will his feelings be returned when Charlotte grows to womanhood?

Aurora of North Manitou Island
by
Donna Winters
Fifth in the series of *Great Lakes Romances*
(Set on North Manitou Island,
Michigan, 1898-1899)
Aurora's wedding Day was far from the glorious event she had anticipated when she put the final stitches in her white satin gown, not with her new husband lying helpless after an accident on stormy Lake Michigan. And when Serilda Anders appeared out of Harrison's past to tend the light and nurse him back to health, Aurora was certain her marriage was doomed before it had ever been properly launched.

Maybe Cad Blackburn was the answer—Cad of the ready wit and the silver tongue. But it wasn't right to accept the safe harbor *he* was offering.

Where was the light that would guide her through these troubled waters?

Bridget of Cat's Head Point
by
Donna Winters
Sixth in the series of *Great Lakes Romances*
(Set in Traverse City and the Leelanau Peninsula
of Michigan, 1899-1900)

When Bridget Richards leaves South Manitou Island to take up residence on Michigan's mainland, she suffers no lack of ardent suitors. Only days after the loss of his first wife, Nat Trevelyn, Bridget's closest friend and the father of a two-year-old son, wants desperately to make her his bride. Kenton McCune, a handsome, wealthy lawyer in Traverse City, showers her with kindness the likes of which she's never known before. And Erik Olson, the son of her employer in Omena, shows her not only the incomparable beauty and romance of a Leelanau summer, but a bravery and affection beyond expectation.

Who will succeed in winning her heart? Or will tragedy swiftly intervene to steal away the promise of lasting happiness and true love?

(Note: The fourth, fifth, and sixth books in the series constitute a trilogy about three sisters in a lightkeeping family in northern Michigan.)

Rosalie of Grand Traverse Bay
by
Donna Winters
Seventh in the series of
Great Lakes Romances
(Set in Traverse City, Michigan and
Forsyth County, North Carolina 1900)

Soon after Rosalie Foxe arrives in Traverse City for the summer of 1900, she stands at the center of a life-changing controversy. Accused of frittering away a gold coin meant for her aunt and uncle's mortgage payment, Rosalie learns they are about to lose their Front Street confectionery and the apartment above which is their home. When Kenton McCune, a handsome, Harvard-trained lawyer comes to their aid, he responds with tart words to Rosalie's claim of innocence. Can her spun-sugar web of sweetness capture his confidence, and his heart?

Meanwhile, Rosalie's horse-crazy younger sister, Vanda Mae, faces problems of her own at Tanglewood, the Foxe family's expansive North Carolina horse farm. Suffering the death of her most cherished mare, the sixteen-year-old seeks comfort in the stable of a lifelong neighbor. But when Willy Jo Winthrop ropes her into his dispute with his daddy, he gets put off the family farm he loves. Will Vanda Mae's prayers be sufficient to settle a yoke of harmony over father and son once again?

(Note: This story is a spin-off from book six.)

Jenny of L'Anse Bay
by
Donna Winters
Special Edition in the series of
Great Lakes Romances
(Set in the Keweenaw Peninsula of
Upper Michigan in 1867)

A raging fire destroys more than Jennifer Crawford's new home . . . it also burns a black hole into her future. To soothe Jennifer's resentful spirit, her parents send her on a trip with their pastor and his wife to the Indian mission at L'Anse Bay. In the wilderness of Michigan's Upper Peninsula, Jennifer soon moves from tourist to teacher, taking over the education of the Ojibway children. Without knowing their language, she must teach them English, learn their customs, and live in harmony with them.

Hawk, son of the Ojibway chief, teaches Jennifer the ways of his tribe. Often discouraged by seemingly insurmountable cultural barriers, Jennifer must also battle danger, death, and the fears that threaten to come between her and the man she loves.

Elizabeth of Saginaw Bay
by
Donna Winters
Pioneer Edition in the series of
Great Lakes Romances
(Set in the Saginaw Valley of Michigan, 1837)

The taste of wedding cake is still sweet in her mouth when Elizabeth Morgan sets out from York State for the new State of Michigan. Her handsome bridegroom, Jacob, has bought land in the frontier town of Riverton in the Saginaw Valley, and Elizabeth dreams of building a home and raising her family in a pleasant community like the one where she grew up. But she hasn't counted on the problems that arise the moment she sets foot on the untamed shore of the Saginaw River.

Riverton is almost non-existent. Her temporary lodgings are crude and infested with insects. And a dangerous disease breaks out among the neighboring Indians, threatening the white folk, as well. Desperately, she seeks a way out of the forest that holds her captive, but God seems to have cut off all possible exits. Surely, He can't mean for her to stay in this raw wilderness?

Sweet Clover: **A Romance of the White City**
Centennial Edition in the series of
Great Lakes Romances

**The World's Columbian Exposition of
1893** brought unmatched excitement and wonder
to Chicago, thus inspiring this innocent tale by
Clara Louise Burnham, first published in 1894.

A Chicago resident from age nine, Burnham
penned her novels in an apartment overlooking
Lake Michigan. Her romance books contain plots
imbued with the customs and morals of a bygone
era—stories that garnered a sizable, loyal reader-
ship in their day.

In *Sweet Clover*, a destitute heroine of
twenty enters a marriage of convenience to ensure
the security and well-being of her fatherless family. Widowed soon after, Clover Bryant Van Tassel
strives to rebuild a lifelong friendship with her late
husband's son. Jack Van Tassel had been her
childhood playmate, and might well have become
her suitor. Believing himself betrayed by both his
father and the girl he once admired, Jack moves far
away from his native city. Then the World's
Columbian Exposition opens, luring him once
again to his old family home.

Hearts warmed by friendship blossom with

affection—in some most surprising ways. Will true love come to all who seek it in the Fair's fabulous White City? The author will keep you guessing till the very end!

Also by Bigwater Publishing

Bigwater Classics™
A series devoted to reprinting literature of the Great Lakes that is currently unavailable to most readers.

Thirty-Three Years Among the Indians
The Story of Mary Sagatoo
Edited by Donna Winters

Volume 1 in the series of *Bigwater Classics*™

In 1863, a young woman in Massachusetts promised to marry a Chippewa Indian from the Saginaw Valley of Michigan. He was a minister whose mission was to bring Christianity to his people in the tiny Indian village of Saganing. Though he later became afflicted with consumption and learned he hadn't long to live, his betrothed would not release him from his promise of marriage. Soon after the newlyweds arrived in

Michigan, this Chippewa Indian extracted a deathbed promise from his new wife.

"Mary . . . will you stay with my people, take my place among them, and try to do for them what I would have done if God had spared my life?" Joseph asked, caressing her hand.

"Oh, Joseph, don't leave me," she begged, "it is so lonesome here!"

"Please make the promise and I shall die happier. Jesus will help you keep it," he said with shortened breath.

Seeing the look of earnestness in Joseph's dark eyes, Mary replied, "I will do as you wish."

Thus began a remarkable woman's thirty-three years among a people about which she knew nothing—years of struggle, hardship, humor, and joy.